W9-DFT-468

WITHOUT ORDERS

WITHOUT ORDERS

by

MARTHA ALBRAND

BOSTON
LITTLE, BROWN AND COMPANY
1943

PRINTED IN THE UNITED STATES OF AMERICA

WITHOUT ORDERS

CHAPTER I

SOMEWHERE in the early dawn a church bell was chiming.

Its thin, melodious sound made Charles stir in his sleep, and in the half-consciousness of awakening he thought, "Ah, it's good to be home again . . . the church bells and the foghorns . . . how I've missed them! Because of them I'll never move uptown. I'll live down here on Washington Square forever. . . ."

A smile fluttered across his face. He yawned, he stretched his whole body, felt the soft linen of the sheets which covered him. Still only half awake, he turned his head and buried his face deeper in the hard square pillow. It felt good and cool. Yet, at the same time, it felt strange. And all of a sudden the smooth linen of the sheets, the soft warmth of the blanket, seemed unfamiliar, too.

He sat up with a start and looked about him. He had never been in this room before. It was perfectly white, its walls and its furniture, like a private room in a hospital. "Hospital," he thought. "Hospital? But I wasn't wounded. Or, was I? Did we try to get away . . . and they caught us . . . sent a few bullets after us?" His hands felt along his body. No bandage. Anywhere. He lifted his legs. All right. No pain, except for the pressure in his head. He sat up. No. He was not wounded. And he didn't feel sick, either.

For a while he just sat and stared. The room was rather small and sparsely furnished but it had central heating and running water and two large windows, their curtains drawn. One easy chair, an enormous, rather old-fashioned chest of drawers, a cupboard, a very plain desk, and the bed in which he had slept with its reading light fixed within easy reach. Several books on the small table next to him.

He pushed the covers back and swung his legs into the room. And again he paused because, in front of him, on a small carpet, stood a pair of slippers, neatly side by side, and across the chair at the end of the bed hung a dark blue silk robe.

His hand reached out for the gown. He had never seen it before. As a matter of fact, he would never have thought of buying anything like that. And none of his friends would ever have presented him with a silk robe. What he was used to wearing was a rather shabby camel's-hair robe which he remembered having left in his apartment on Washington Square to wait for him till the war was over.

He felt the blood thudding at the back of his head. He couldn't think clearly. He walked quickly on bare feet across the tiled flooring to the washbasin in the corner, turned on the cold water and slapped it into his face with both hands. Then he grabbed a towel and, drying himself with the one hand, tore aside the curtain of the window next to him with the other. There were iron bars in front of the window.

So this was a prison!

Through the bars he could see the proud tall points of high and many-year-old cypresses, a single cedar tree, the dark shiny green of the leaves of summer magnolias not yet in bloom and, among them, camellias, camellia trees laden with white, pink and dark red blossoms. A beautifully laid-out and very old Italian park, and, at its far end, flanked by tall cypresses and oleander bushes, one of the little chapels that, in this country, went with a big estate. . . .

He stepped back and put his hand up to his aching head. Italy. Yes, of course. Italy. They had taken him to Italy, him and Jim and Dell. Prisoners of war. Goddam bloody luck! They had been thrown into a camp for several days as soon as they had arrived in port – which one he didn't know because they had been blindfolded – then they had been herded into a train, had arrived at another camp to wait there for further shunting about – to be sent to work in a factory or, if they were lucky, out into the country to help farm it, or, less lucky, to another prison camp somewhere inland. Yesterday . . . yes, yesterday, an old sergeant had again taken down all their data, put them through a lot of questions, and, later, the guard had brought them something to eat and had told them that they would be sent away tomorrow, "*domani,*" or "*dopo domani,*" the day after tomorrow.

Jim . . . Dell . . . Where were they? What had happened to them? Somehow they had never thought they would be separated. They had become friends during the short time they had spent together.

Charles dropped the curtain, strode across the room and tried the door. It was locked.

He fell back on his bed. Prisoner, all right. But where? He began to smile and shrugged his shoulders. No use making a rumpus. He'd find out shortly, anyhow.

He lay very still, trying to compose himself, but nagging curiosity made his whole body ache with impatience. If only he could think clearly. His head felt horrible with the dull, heavy pain which had settled itself now above his eyes.

"Escape," he thought.

They had talked escape whenever they had had a chance during the last weeks. Escape — in the prison yard which had been nothing but a piece of fenced-in deadly desert, well guarded; escape — when they had been herded onto the boat; escape, when they had landed; escape, when they had been put on the train with no idea as to where it was taking them; escape . . .

He knew Italy. He knew Switzerland, and the trails through the mountains, and the shores of the Lago Maggiore. Once they knew where they were, they would try.

"Snap out of it!" he said aloud to himself. "You don't know where you are."

He turned his attention to the books on the small table next to his bed. He reached out for them, not intending to read, just for something to do, anything to take his mind off his fruitless thoughts. And then, again, he started. Plato's *Republic,* in English; Machiavelli's *Principe,* and an English-Italian dictionary. His nervous tension broke into a storm of laughter. He laughed so hard that his whole body shook. Wherever he was, whoever was keeping him prisoner here certainly had a definite philosophic and political opinion. And how thoughtful to add the dictionary!

Plato. Great God! It made him think of Princeton and long bull sessions; it made him think of an evening shortly before the United States had declared war when they had discussed world problems and what could be done and how Arthur had insisted . . . He hadn't read Plato since he was twenty and that was almost fourteen years ago . . .

Just as he had started to read, he heard a key turn in the lock of his door. The book slipped onto the floor and again he sat up straight, his body tense, all its blood hammering in his veins.

"*Buongiorno,*" said a man's voice. "I hope you have slept well, *Signore?* You seemed very tired last night. Do you want your breakfast up here in your room or do you feel well enough to go downstairs?"

"Prisoner of war," thought Charles. "Breakfast in bed?"

He stared at the man who was walking towards the window and now pulled the curtains aside properly, as Charles had not had the patience to do, by their cords. There was nothing extraordinary about this man except that he seemed unusually tall and strong, and he wore a quaint sort of suit, not unlike a uniform, yet definitely not a uniform – dark gray trousers with a jacket to match. The jacket was buttoned up all the way in the front. But that wasn't what startled Charles. It was the attitude of the man. The man behaved as if he knew him, knew him well, not with the indifferent manner a well-trained servant might show toward an unknown guest, but with a certain familiarity in spite of his politeness. This served to confuse Charles far more than the unexpectedness of his surroundings or the books on his table.

"I'll shave you now," the man said, and moved a straight chair in front of the basin.

"Who are you?" asked Charles. "What's your name?"

The man turned around and smiled at him, a wide, flashy, artificial smile.

"Why, Signor da Ponte," he said, "you know just as well as I that my name is Bruno."

Charles cleared his throat. "Bruno," he said, "you are making a mistake and you know it. You don't know me and I don't know you. Up till the moment you entered, I didn't even know you existed. I am not Signor da Ponte. I am Charles J. Barrett."

"Of course," answered Bruno, taking some utensils out of one of his big side-pockets and spreading them on the basin. "Will you kindly come over here, Signor da Ponte?"

"Barrett."

The man said nothing.

Charles reached for the dressing gown and this time he stepped into the slippers. And, again, he stopped in surprise. They almost fitted him. He glanced at Bruno, but the man wasn't paying any attention to him. "He's crazy," thought Charles, and sat down.

"I am sorry," said Bruno, "there is very little soap left. I can't make a good job of shaving any more. If we get permission, we will have an electric shaving machine and then you will be allowed to shave yourself."

His big, strong hands handled the razor expertly.

"Bruno," said Charles, "where am I?" He looked at the man's blunt face, which had gone completely blank, and corrected himself. "I mean, could you tell where I am?"

"Where you have always been," said Bruno, walking away from him to the cupboard. He opened its door and came back, underwear and a suit over his arm.

"There you are, Signor da Ponte. Do you want me to help you?"

"My name is Barrett," said Charles. "Charles J. Barrett. *Barretto,* without the *o.* And I have been dressing myself ever since I was four years old."

"Hush," said the man. "Now, don't get excited. There is nothing to get excited about. Just calm yourself. If you don't want me to help you dress today, it's all right with me."

Charles heard the door click. This time it was not locked.

He stared at the clothes. They were by no means new, a little old-fashioned in cut and material, but immaculately clean. And as with the dressing-gown and slippers – they almost fitted him. He put his hand in one of the pockets and found a pipe – his pipe; a watch, and a handkerchief with the initials V.dP. How in the world did his pipe and watch get into the pocket of a jacket he had never worn before? Someone must have put them there, someone who had brought him here.

When he was ready he opened the door. Because his room was the last one on the floor, a wide corridor spread out before him – tiled, as so many passageways in old Italian castles and houses were. At its end, a long staircase swung down to the lower floor.

As he stood there, hesitating, an old man came out of one of the rooms, stopped short to look at him, and smiled – "Ah! *Buongiorno.* Coming down for breakfast? It does get tiresome to be alone all the time, doesn't it?" – and passed him and went on and down the stairs. Halfway down he stopped, his face turned up. "You see," he said, "if you would just believe in God, it would be so much easier for you, for all of us. This, now, that is going on all over the world is the Great Flood.

And we will all be drowned. Excuse me for bothering you." He bowed politely and continued downstairs.

Charles stood where he had stopped and looked about him. From below he could hear voices, and when he leaned over the heavily carved bannisters, he could see two men, dressed as Bruno had been, moving about.

A hand touched his shoulder and he swung around to face a man whose white outfit showed him to be a doctor, a man of about forty, with a clear-cut, rather intelligent face.

"Good morning, Signor Vittorio," the doctor said. "You certainly look well today. Bruno told me you had a good night."

"*Dottore,*" said Charles, "may I speak to you? In my room, in your office, anywhere?"

"Why, certainly," said the doctor, and made a gesture with his hand to indicate the way to a door on the same floor.

Behind him Charles entered a small office which smelled strongly of disinfectant. As soon as the door was shut, Charles said, "Look, *Dottore*. There is obviously a mistake somewhere. I mean, all of you are mistaking me for somebody I certainly am not. I am Charles J. Barrett."

The doctor sat down and folded his hands between the insides of his knees. With his head and back slightly bowed, he looked as if nothing whatsoever could ruffle him.

"Charles Barrett. Born –"

"Born in May," the doctor interrupted, "the seventh of May, if I remember right, in Tulsa, Oklahoma, on Denver Street."

Charles sat down and breathed more freely. Everything seemed to be O.K. at last. This man knew who he was. "Correct!" he said, helpfully, and now he smiled because he felt so relieved and because he couldn't think why it had made him so nervous to be treated by two people he had never seen before as if they had known him for years.

"Where am I?" he said. "Or is it a military secret? How did I get here? Could you . . . would you tell me?"

The doctor lifted his head and looked at him. Behind the sharp glasses, his eyes were cold, almost cruel.

"You are not feeling as well as I thought you were, are you?" he said. "And you were so much better. I am afraid we will have to continue with the treatments." He shook his head. "You were so much better," he repeated, and it sounded quite sincere.

"I don't know what you mean," Charles said. "I tell you, you are making a mistake! I've never seen you before! You're not going to try to tell me you know me?"

The doctor spread his arms wide and let his hands rest on each side of the chair. "I've known you ever since you were eighteen years old."

"You're crazy!" said Charles, and he breathed deeply to force himself to keep quiet. "A month ago I was fighting with my outfit in North Africa. I and two comrades were protecting an ambulance, when all of a sudden we were taken prisoner by an advance group of Italians."

He saw the doctor smile and asked, irritated, "What are you smiling at? It's true, I tell you. I am a prisoner of war. You believe me, don't you?"

"My dear Vittorio da Ponte," said the doctor. "That is the story you have been telling me for the last twenty-four years, on and off, ever since you came here. The war you are speaking about is the last war."

For a second Charles was speechless. He wanted to shout at the doctor, he wanted to jump up, to cross over to where this man sat so quietly and patiently in his chair; he wanted to grab him as if he were a small dog, lift him up by the collar and shake him. But his whole body seemed paralyzed. He thought rapidly and clearly, he thought of the words he wanted to say, but his tongue refused to formulate them. His brain had lost the control that made his body act. After what seemed a long while to him, he breathed deeply again, and he could feel the air hitting his lungs with a small stab of pain.

"*Dottore,*" he said, his voice dark and low with the effort to keep it steady. "I have never been in a war before. This . . . this has been my first experience . . . these last three months. I was born in nineteen hundred and eight. I am not quite thirty-five years old. The first World War ended in 1918." He tried to smile, to win the doctor's reasonableness. "It would have been quite impossible for a ten-year-old boy . . ."

He broke off. The doctor's face remained a blank. He looked right now as Bruno had looked, slightly bored and absolutely disinterested.

"*Dottore* —" said Charles, again.

"Your record shows that you were born in 1900."

"The record of Signor Vittorio da Ponte or whoever it is you want to mistake me for!"

"You are Signor Vittorio da Ponte."

It was said so quietly that the atmosphere in the small white room which smelled of medication seemed charged with uncanniness. Charles stood up. Directly opposite him, above a little washbasin, hung a mirror. Only now, as he walked over to it, did he remember that there had been no mirror in his room. Now he looked at himself. Right then he needed that look more than anything else in the world.

It was a clear little mirror, cut out of crystal, and it gave him the confirmation he wanted so badly. There was his face as he had always known it – a little more haggard than it used to be, with a high and slightly rounded forehead, the little scar above his left eye almost lost in a deep line; his eyes chestnut brown, with deep shadows about them now; his nose a little crooked there, where a baseball bat had once hit him; the prominent and dominating jaw with that silly dimple right bang in the middle of his chin . . . His face, Charles J. Barrett's face, the face of his father and grandfather before him. He hadn't looked at himself the way he did now for a long, long time. Once, when he was sixteen, and the girl he adored had turned him down for reasons he couldn't understand, he had fled to the mirror, so horribly embarrassed and pitifully unsure of himself. After all, maybe she was right, and he did look like a freckled, lanky, awkward brat. And then, again, when he had won a Rockefeller scholarship – two years in Europe – he had looked at himself, proud and happy that he had succeeded. And two years ago: his first "first night" on Broadway; his mother had come from Oklahoma and had insisted that he wear dinner clothes . . .

A great assuredness came over him. He was

Lieutenant Charles J. Barrett, American prisoner of war, and he knew it. When he turned, he caught the doctor's glance. The man had been watching every single move he had made, but now he pretended that he had just been staring into space.

"What is your name, *Dottore?*" he asked, and sat down again.

"Pederazzini." The doctor stuck his hand into his pocket and drew it out again, holding a small cigaret case made of the hard-pressed polished leather Italy had been famous for before the war had started claiming it for boots. He opened it. It contained a single cigaret. The doctor looked at it pensively, then he broke it into two parts and offered one to Charles on his palm.

"*Grazie tante,*" said Charles, with sincere gratitude.

The doctor struck a match and reached across his desk. The thin paper, out of which some tobacco had fallen, caught a little flame. "Damn them!" thought Charles suddenly. "We had at least a hundred cigarets with us when they came upon us. They took them. I think they were happier about the cigarets than about having taken some prisoners."

He heard the doctor say something.

"*Scusi?*" he said politely.

"Absent-minded, again," said Pederazzini, and

then his voice came sterner. "Snap out of it, *Signore*. At once! You have been playing an American called Charles Barrett on and off now since you first came here. But for the last half year you have behaved absolutely normally. For almost six months now, you have ceased trying to escape into a different personality when you got tired of your own. This is the first serious relapse. I feel that you are normal enough for me to talk to you this way. We had already seriously thought of releasing you in the very near future. But now, after this setback . . ." He shrugged his shoulders and sighed.

Charles didn't answer. He stared out of the window, which, like the one in his room, was barred. He had come to a decision – if the doctor and the man, Bruno, took the liberty of not paying any attention to the things he said which they didn't like him to say, then he had the same privilege. He would not pay any attention to what they said that he didn't like.

"Did you hear what I said?"

"No," barked Charles, all of a sudden in English. "God damn you! Why can't you see reason? Just wait! I'll go right on insisting that I'm Charles J. Barrett from Tulsa, Oklahoma, till I'm blue in the face!"

"You have certainly succeeded in learning English," said Pederazzini. "I can remember when you came here how you insisted on English primers so that you could study the language you liked so much."

"You can?" said Charles. "That's very interesting. Before I came here I didn't know a word of English, did I?"

"A little, naturally," the doctor said, and began to play with a fountain pen in front of him on his desk. "You had learned a little in school, but your studies were interrupted when you volunteered."

"I volunteered?" said Charles, and Pederazzini looked up at him. He took off his glasses and Charles saw that Pederazzini's eyes without his glasses had an almost naked glance, dark, deep, sad eyes.

"Yes. Of course, you did." There was something like respect and kindliness in his voice, now. "You were a mere boy. But when your father was killed in the Dolomites in the fight on the Col di Lana, you decided to avenge him."

Father, thought Charles. He won't know where I am. He'll try to find out. The Red Cross . . . And, like a flash, a memory of childhood days came back to him. He had been very little at the time and already asleep when he had suddenly been awakened by the ringing of the old-fashioned wall telephone. Dad had taken the call, jumping out of bed in his old-fashioned nightgown, not bothering to put on slippers, great corns showing on his left and right little toes, there where the greasy, heavy field boots had rubbed them. Oil. They had reached sand sooner than had been expected and he had been allowed to get up. His father had grabbed his hand and together they had raced through the night, through mud and dust, till they had reached the drilling rig. He could feel it now, sitting opposite Dr. Pederazzini – the excitement and romance of that hour when dreams and hard labor had been personified in the rich, acrid, satisfactory odor of the heavy oil sand.

"And where did you say I went to school?" he asked. "I mean, before I volunteered."

I could tell you, he thought. I went to Lawrenceville, and then, when oil prices collapsed, I worked my way through college. Because I was a Barrett, and the Barretts have never been afraid of work.

"You went to the Jesuit school in Verona," Dr. Pederazzini said. "A very good school. Brother Anselmo –"

"Verona," said Charles, and he began to smile.

Verona. Oh, yes. He had lived there before he had moved on to Venice and Florence and Rome. He had lived in the little town of Romeo and Juliet, in an old, one-story-high house on the River

Adige, but he hadn't found Juliet there. Nor anywhere, after Jean had died.

"You were born there," said the doctor. "Your father's estate was just south of Verona. Your mother, Katherine, died shortly after . . . after you came here."

My mother is alive, thought Charles. She is a tiny woman who, when Dad first took her out to Oklahoma, was afraid of the Indians. It wasn't a state then. She comes from New Orleans and loves speaking the Latin languages, although she has never been in Europe. She has never seen Verona, except on the picture postcards I sent her.

Now he felt almost relaxed, he felt almost kindly disposed towards the doctor who had just told him another man's life story, wanting him to believe it was his own. If he could just keep quiet, if he could just keep on treating this whole damn mistake as a huge joke, he would eventually succeed in convincing the doctor of his story . . . or he would find a way of escape.

"Verona," said the doctor. "You remember Verona, Signor da Ponte. You remember your father, Francesco da Ponte. He was one of the Venetian da Pontes. His hair was that famous Titian red that can only be found in Venice. Yours — " and it sounded regretful — "yours is just ordinary brown except when the sun hits it as it does now and gives it a tinge of red. You spent your summer vacations in Venice."

Charles didn't answer.

Venice . . . Oh, yes. He remembered Venice. The first time he had gone there not knowing that Italy's second Caruso was singing on the Piazza San Marco – an outdoor concert. Gigli – his powerful voice sounding all over the town, the lagoon and the canals . . . And not a room to be found anywhere, not in the biggest hotels, not in the smallest *alberghis*. He had spent the night in the *barca* he had hired on his arrival – his gondolier humming the melodies of Gigli's music, pushing the paddle with his body moving rhythmically in hundred-year-old fashion, his muscles trained and bred for this profession; and, when he had finally grown sleepy, leaning a little more heavily on the wooden paddle, but still pushing it . . . And the people dressed in their old and glamorous costumes, dancing in the narrow streets and across the curved bridges and on the *piazzettas* . . . And Fenice, the little restaurant opposite the old Opera House – one was permitted to go into the kitchen, lift the covers from the pots, and taste the food before one ordered a certain dish . . . And Jimmy's American Bar, not far from it, where the motorboats came in from the Lido to discharge the guests, foreigners . . . He had not been a foreigner. He not only had learned to speak their language, he had understood them.

"Sometimes your mother would stop in Abano to take the cure there," the doctor said.

Abano . . . where the hot healing waters spurted out of the ground and people sat in their back yards and boiled eggs in the little puddles that the water breaking through the soil would form. Verona, Venice and Abano . . . Yes, he had been there. As a matter of fact, he had been all over Italy: on foot and by car, on trains and by bicycle. Even to Sicily and Calabria. . . .

Charles leaned back.

Naples . . . Naples, too. When had it been? In '33 or '34. When he had taken a boat across to Greece, past Rhodes. Sometime, when the war was over and the peace won, he would fall in love, he would take a boat, one of those little white luxury steamers that used to leave from Venice for the island of Rhodes, and take his beloved there. But that time he had continued through Palestine into Syria and Iraq and on to Persia. The British were building the oil pipeline from Teheran to Haifa, and his job had been to cover it.

His eyes wandered and stopped at the window. Through its bars he could now see several people walking in the wide garden. Some of them wore bluish-gray suits which did not fit too well, and here and there he could see men dressed like Bruno.

"Verona," Pederazzini repeated. "You were an only child and you were named after your grandfather."

Suddenly Charles realized that the doctor was patiently but determinedly trying to bring back memories, trying to pull him out of the personality of Charles Barrett which, as he had just mentioned, Vittorio da Ponte had escaped into; believing that Vittorio da Ponte had done it again, working on him as a psychiatrist, impressing upon him things from the past which he, presumably, had forgotten. Dr. Pederazzini was sure that he, Charles J. Barrett, was Vittorio da Ponte, born in Verona, who had been here for almost twenty-five years. Here. Where?

"This is a hospital," he said sharply, "and the men in the gray suits out there are attendants."

The doctor nodded. Again he reached for his cigaret case, snapped it open as if he wanted to convince himself that the cigaret he had just smoked had really been his last, and then, with obvious disgust, pushed it back into the pocket of his white jacket.

"A prison hospital?"

"Everybody here is a prisoner. I think you can

call it that." Pederazzini smiled vaguely. There was something unbelievably sad in his face.

The telephone at the left of the small writing desk shrilled. The doctor lifted the receiver, listened intently, asked one or two strictly professional questions and then said: "I'll be right up. Slip him into a jacket."

The word seemed to fill the small white room, seemed to swallow all the air that had been there for them to breathe. Charles jumped up, strode across the floor toward the window and threw it wide open. He pressed his face against the strong iron bars, feeling the coldness of the metal like a tender hand on his hot cheeks. Up till now he had somehow believed that his case was simple, just a case of mistaken identity which would be cleared up in a short while – a day, or a week – it might even take a month; had believed that by some silly error he had been sent to a hospital of some kind. Now he knew where he was.

He said, "This is an institution for the mentally ill . . . a lunatic asylum?" His voice was scarcely audible.

The doctor picked up his glasses from the blotter where he had put them a moment ago and within a second his face had again become a mask of cold indifference. "Yes," he said – and, after a little while during which he put several instruments in a case: "My dear *Signore*. You'd better go up to your room or take a stroll in the park. My time is up."

Charles leapt across the room and caught hold of the doctor's right shoulder. "I am not crazy," he said. "I am not crazy!" Suddenly he was breathless. "I tell you, I am not crazy!"

The doctor didn't answer. He just looked at him. And across his face was clearly written what he thought – "That, *Signore,* is what all crazy people say. They are forever trying to convince one that they are normal."

When had he been frantic last? As a child, when his colored mammy Delia had threatened him with the Indians who would come by night and get him? Or the day when the plane Jeanie had taken was overdue for six hours till the news came that it had crashed in the California mountains? Or when, covering a big fire in Chicago's downtown district, they had slaved for hours helping to put it out; and then had had to give up a little two-story frame house which had blown up like dry straw, in which they knew two people and a dog were still upstairs? . . . He was frantic now.

The doctor – of all persons in the world, he was the only one that mattered! The doctor had to believe him! He had to convince the doctor! He had to!

"I tell you, I am a case of mistaken identity. I am Lieutenant Charles J. Barrett, prisoner of war. What date is today? The fourth. Only yesterday I was in a camp, in a lousy little camp. Lousy! Filthy! We had nothing but some awful soup . . . Dell Marsh and Jim Provin. They both had diarrhea. *Dottore!*"

Strange that one didn't get frantic when one knew one was facing death or drowning, when the ship one happened to be on was hit by a torpedo, a shell aimed precisely or just a stray one. One was afraid – perhaps. He had been, sometimes. But not frantic, never frantic with the realization of utter helplessness, dependent on the good will of other people. Did other people have good will? People were essentially good. No. People were essentially bad. Why, otherwise, would laws be necessary? He had to convince the doctor!

"I've been fighting in North Africa. I am not crazy. All I want you to do, Dr. Pederazzini, is to write a letter . . ."

He stopped suddenly, caught his breath and went on.

"We landed only yesterday morning, I don't know where, but you can find out. Just ask the military officials – I don't know what they call them here – and they will tell you that a prisoner, Lieutenant Charles J. Barrett, born in Tulsa, Oklahoma, with the American forces in North Africa, was taken prisoner by the Italians with two other men . . ."

"Let go of my arm," said the doctor. "I am in a hurry. You were not very co-operative today, Signor Vittorio. I am very disappointed. After the good progress you made . . ."

"Somebody's slipped up somewhere! I'm not Vittorio da Ponte! I'm telling you I'm Lieutenant Charles J. Barrett. We were supposed to be sent to some destination which of course I don't know . . ."

He saw the doctor make a move. He heard him say, "Calm yourself."

"Calm myself?" he shouted. "Calm myself? What would you do in my place, Dr. Pederazzini? You go and volunteer and do your bit, you count on not coming back alive, on becoming a cripple if fate wants it that way, on such lousy luck as to be taken prisoner to slave for people you despise or to spend years in a prison camp, but you don't count on finding yourself in an asylum being treated like a loony! You don't figure on mistakes like that! What would you do if you were in my place, completely sane, as sane as only an American can be, and you found yourself . . ."

"I would calm myself. First of all I would calm myself. Calm yourself," he repeated.

The door opened. Bruno stood there. Charles had not heard him knock.

"Signor Vittorio is very excited," the doctor said. "You'd better take him up to his room. If he doesn't behave himself, give him a hypo. If that doesn't help, you know what you have to do."

He moved quickly away from Charles and across to the door.

Charles went after him. He mustn't go. Not now! Not yet! It took him two steps to cover the distance for which Pederazzini had needed seven. He reached out, intending only to hold the doctor back; but like a flash, Bruno's arms were around him – immensely strong arms, like iron chains pressing around his chest, holding him mercilessly. His feet lost ground, he slipped to the floor, and Bruno's arms were still around him.

For a minute Charles sat very still. From outside the window he could hear someone talking in a whining complaining voice. And he could hear the sharp, rhythmic click-clack with which some patient, some harmless idiot, moved his long scissors as he cut the hedge.

Somewhere there must be a fence. Somewhere there must be a way of escape. . . .

He moved quickly, trying to shake off Bruno by a surprise movement. But Bruno was on his guard.

Charles felt his arms bent back, back, till the pain made him wince.

"Now don't try any funny business," said Bruno. "You never used to give me so much trouble, Signor Vittorio. Why start now?"

"I am not crazy," said Charles. "Bruno. Why, why do you pretend that you have seen me before, that you know me? All right. I've been sent here by some error. Why can't you treat me like a new patient instead of putting on this show of having known me?"

"I don't know what you are talking about," said Bruno, and to his surprise, Charles saw him smile, a wide, broad, genuine grin.

"I tell you what's the matter with you," said Charles, feeling the pressure on his arms relaxing. "You . . . you are crazy."

"Sure," said Bruno, "sure, Signor Vittorio. And I don't mind it a bit. The shape the world is in now, the crazy people are running around free and the sane ones are behind bars. This is not such a bad place after all, and maybe we are lucky. Who knows? You'd better come along now without giving me any more trouble."

Charles felt much quieter now, undoubtedly as a result of the hypodermic which Bruno had after all felt obliged to give him. Charles pushed the sleeve of his shirt up to his elbow and looked at the tiny red mark where the needle had penetrated his skin. It made him think of all the shots they had given him before they had sailed from the United States, and of how rotten they had made him feel. This shot, now, made him feel good. A little light-headed, though.

Bruno came in carrying a tray. He put a cup of tea and some *grissinis* – little sticks of bread – on the desk. "Here you are," he said. "And when you have eaten, you are free to do whatever you like. You can go down and help cut bandages or take a walk," and he left without another word.

Charles drank the tea. It tasted horrible, even more awful than tea used to taste before the war. He broke one of the long, small sticks of bread. It was hard, like stone. He dunked it into his cup and munched it. In between bites he spoke to himself, "I must not lose my nerve. I must not lose my temper. I must not get violent. If I get violent, they will put me into a strait-jacket or throw me into a padded cell and I won't ever get a chance to look around."

He listened to his own voice as intently as he would have listened to a voice from the other world. It was his voice, all right, a low yet clear voice, a voice that carried well. Because of this voice and his knowledge of languages he had been working in Intelligence, "contacting" foreign countries, until he had decided that he would like to do more than fill a job which so many others could do just as well, maybe even better, with New York full of people of all nationalities as it was today.

New York . . . He hadn't been homesick for New York when he had been abroad before, because he knew it was his for the taking, that it was entirely up to him if he wanted to see it again. He hadn't longed to be back when he had been put through his basic training; he hadn't longed for New York when they had marched through the desert convoyed by planes and tanks, because then he had been marching under a mercilessly blazing sun in order that he or some other American might go back when it was over — to make the seven seas fit for everyone to sail, to clear the skies so that everyone could take advantage of the twentieth century's inventions, those inventions which seemed to have been sponsored by the angels to make life easier and more agreeable, and had then been taken over by the devils for destruction. But now, here, locked up in a lunatic asylum without the slightest chance of escape, he was desperately homesick for New York.

He opened the drawer of the table, looking for paper and pencil, but what he found was a batch of photographs. He spread them out in front of him. Some were just ordinary enlargements, six by nine, some were portraits. One, a little faded, showed a man in the picturesque uniform of the Bersaglieri, three-quarter face, the black cock-feathers on one side of the large brimmed hat swooping across his shoulders. A good-looking man with a typical Roman jaw and a proud, dominating nose. At the bottom there was an inscription, "*To my son, Vittorio. February 1916.* FRANCESCO DA PONTE, *Capitano.*"

The next one showed Signora Caterina da Ponte. She was sitting in a straight chair, a small and beautiful woman, her black hair parted in the middle, the little curls falling behind her ears, her face almost saintly in its expression. She was dressed in white lace and in her arms she held an infant in old-fashioned swaddling clothes.

Then there was the photograph of a large white house built in the style of the Renaissance, and in front of it a fountain – three dolphins holding an oval marble basin aloft on their curved tails.

Why was this house familiar to him? Why?

He put the pictures down and, biting his lips, remained to stare at them. He knew this house, knew the balcony, obviously a later addition, spanning the whole of the second floor; knew the large, lovely gate of artfully worked wrought-iron.

Why, of course! He had seen it on one of his many trips from Verona to Venice.

He pushed the pictures back into the drawer. No good looking at them. No good thinking of them. He was Charles J. Barrett.

He opened the door and walked along the corridor and down the staircase. As earlier in the morning, he heard the sound of voices from downstairs. Then, drawing closer, he saw through an open door a large hall, in which, under the surveillance of two wardens, several people were working, cutting bandages . . . The more harmless cases, he thought, passing the door quickly, as if afraid a warden might see him and ask him to come in and help. The terrible shyness of a completely sane person towards those he knows are no longer masters of their minds swept over him. Just then a sister in the gray colorless habit of the Misericordia nuns came out into the lobby and bent her head to him in silent greeting.

"Could you show me how to get into the park?" he asked.

She lifted her head. Under the ugly hood her face seemed the first lovely thing he had seen in a long time.

"It is a beautiful day," she said, and unfolded her hands, pointing reluctantly, as if it embarrassed her to possess hands that were so startlingly beautiful, as if all she should have and be able to show were her soul.

"To the right? Thank you."

He wanted to ask her if she, too, believed she had seen him before, but she moved away so quickly that she was gone before he had come to this decision. He turned and walked across the tiled floor of the large entrance hall where, at the far end, he could see the portal.

It was locked. But in its left wing there was a small window which opened easily enough.

"You can go out if you want to," a voice behind him said, and only then did he see that next to the door was a small iron grille, behind which a warden sat at his desk.

"Have a nice walk, Signor Vittorio."

Charles saw the man's foot move, and the big door in front of him swung open noiselessly. An electric Sesame, he thought. I must remember that. Somewhere at the foot of that desk is a button which works the door.

Five large steps led down into the park. Charles didn't move. He stood on the first wide step and stared into the sky. Like an immense blue bell the sky hung above the landscape and in its dark deep blue there was something transparent. It had a light all its own, a light which no sky in any other country held. Suddenly he began to run, taking the last four steps in one big jump, turning abruptly to face in the other direction. But the high, sober building of the asylum barred the view. As if his body had ceased to exist, as if his legs had become divining rods, he moved automatically to the left, till, all of a sudden, he found himself at the back of the asylum where some patients were working in a vegetable garden. He didn't see the rows of early asparagus, nor the high iron fence which enclosed everything, nor the flat country all around dabbed with the already dusty green of olive trees. He only saw, far away, the graceful outlines of the blue Alban Mountains.

"Rome," he whispered. "Rome. I am near Rome."

He stood for a long time, his hands buried in his pockets, his whole body motionless. Rome. Only above Rome did the sky have its own light.

After a little while he turned back and into the park again. So he was near Rome. Whom had he known in Rome? The Browns, of course, foreign correspondents for the *Tribune,* and a whole crowd of reporters: French, British, Swedish, Swiss, and many Italians . . . Pietro and Cleme and Luisa and Fumasoli and Giulio. What had happened to them? Where were they now? Fighting, fighting their own kind of battle. He would write to them all. Any one of them could identify him if . . . if he could manage to smuggle the letter out. But there must be some connection with the outside world . . . a milkman, a butcher. They couldn't have everything right here. Or did the institution own a farm where they produced all that was necessary for the maintenance of the patients? Then a servant, or a cook – someone!

Suddenly he felt exhausted with excitement. He fell onto one of the benches which stood at regular distances along the garden paths.

"*Permesso?*" said a voice very close to him.

An elderly man of rather stout build stood directly in front of him, leaning on a cane. Charles hadn't seen him coming. He had been dreaming with his eyes wide open, trying to recall memories of the months he had spent in this city, of his friends of happier days.

"*Sì, sì,*" he said, a little annoyed at the disturbance. He glanced across the path. As far as he could see, every other bench was empty. He had forgotten the Latin characteristic which shuns loneliness as a wild bronco shuns a hurdle and would inevitably look for company, on the street, in the little sidewalk cafés, at the best restaurants.

"You are very kind," said the man, "thank you," and he bowed politely before he sat down.

Instinctively Charles moved, forgetting for a second where he was, and immediately the man said, "Don't be nervous. I am harmless. They wouldn't let me come out here all by myself if I were not. Don't you think so?"

Now, for the first time, Charles noticed the man's face. It was a good face, with sharp, outspoken features, with an intelligent thin-lipped mouth and penetrating dark eyes.

But I know him! thought Charles. I know that face. Where did I see it? When?

"Have we ever met before?" he asked, and he wouldn't have been surprised to hear, "Why, certainly, Signor Vittorio. We have been friends now for a great many years."

But the man shook his head.

"No," he said. "Never, as far as I can remember."

For the first time since he had awakened in his strange surroundings, Charles felt almost happy. It was just like going to the mirror for assurance. "But then, of course," said the man, "I only believe in what I see and feel and not in what I am told I should believe. You see, I am a little crazy," and he pointed to his forehead.

CHAPTER II

CHARLES began to laugh. What a wonderful line! To consider oneself crazy because one refused to think what others wanted one to think. Then, all of a sudden, he heard himself laugh. He stopped abruptly and sat petrified. Never before had he been conscious of his own laughter. It didn't ring true to him. It . . . it sounded hysterical . . . artificial . . . crazy!

"The *Signore* doesn't feel well?" the man asked, looking at him in a strange, anxious way. "Do you want me to call one of the attendants to take you back to the house?"

"No. No, thank you. *Grazie molto,*" said Charles. He leaned back, feeling the hard wood press his spine just above his shoulderblades.

"I am perfectly all right," he said, and when the other man's glance remained fixed on his face, he added, "I have been in the war . . . you know."

He was watching himself now, listening to his

voice echoing back into his ears, watching his own words to see whether they made sense.

"I understand. I understand," said the man. "War is an awful thing. I was in the war myself. But I hate wars; as a true Italian, I hate war. Someone should stop it. Someone should stop all the people making war." He put his arms out, his hand touched Charles's sleeve. "Don't you agree, *Signore?*"

"*Sicuro, sicuro,*" said Charles. "Certainly, I do." He turned his head once again to face the man next to him. He looked almost childish now and his eyes had a pleading intensity.

He's a harmless old fellow, he thought, a childish little man. . . . And then once again the humor of the situation overwhelmed him and his lips broke into a grin. He couldn't help it, because that was the way he was made. He could always see the funny side of things. Some people had called this quality of his "typically American." Well, maybe it was, at least, as far as concerned the Anglo-Saxon mind that hated to dramatize anything, that was so wholeheartedly for understatement.

What a fantastic situation this was! This poor idiot talking about how horrible wars were and that one should stop them and he . . . What a play it would make! he thought. I couldn't have thought it up. It would have been too incredible a situation. But funny – funny as hell! And true, too. Why, I should write a play about it, he thought. That would give me something to do while I am here, and that would help me to keep going. There is one point, though, I would have to stress – that it is not the confinement, not the barred windows, not the fenced-in surroundings that make you jittery, but the fact that everyone you talk to takes it for granted that you're cracked.

Next to him the man babbled on.

"I didn't choose a military career. I inherited it. You see, as a farmer's son mostly becomes a farmer, an officer's son will follow in his father's footsteps. And it is a nice profession – discipline and honor accompany it. But they should not be used in warfare. Soldiers should be there, all right, but not to fight . . . not to fight . . . To keep the peace. In that sense Plato wanted guardians for the safety of the state . . ."

Plato? Plato's *Republic* lay next to his bed in his room on the second floor.

"What is your name?" Charles asked abruptly, almost rudely.

This time the man smiled. "I have chosen to forget it," he said. "Just call me Pietro. Everybody around here calls me Pietro."

He began to rub his chin as though it were all a huge joke. Two spots of red colored his cheeks.

They stood out on his pallid yellow complexion like a dab of rouge carelessly put on.

"You come from Lombardy, don't you? You speak like the people there." He got up, moved back a few steps and gave Charles another of his scrutinizing looks. "Yet there is something that . . . It's the way you move your body," he went on, sitting down again.

Charles said, "I am an American. But I have lived in Italy for almost two years. In Verona and Rome, before I went to war."

Pietro accepted this without the slightest sign of surprise. "I speak English, too," he said. "How do you do, Mister? It is a real pleasure to meet you."

Two people followed by an attendant passed their bench. Nobody paid any attention to them. "I like your people," Pietro went on. "I visited your country several years ago. But I don't know very much about it. I only saw Washington and New York. At that time . . . Well, never mind. You see, we Italians are awfully indifferent towards politics. That is how HE got in and has been able to remain where he is now. We had been living such, well, such democratic lives for such a long time that we didn't think anything could really make a difference. Mazzini, Garibaldi and Cavour's spirit seemed to be too deeply anchored in our people's hearts for anything to ever uproot it."

He was wearing a dark gray sweater under his jacket of nondescript color, which left his neck bare. It was a surprisingly strong neck, a young neck, with hardly any lines, no flesh which shouldn't be there, with a strong Adam's apple moving under the thin, pallid skin. It was a military neck.

"Did you ever meet Count Sforza? He is exiled, you know. He wrote a splendid book, *The Soul of Italy.* You should read it. Everyone should read it who wants to know what we Italians are really like."

Again he jumped up, this time stamping his foot angrily on the gravel path. "How I hate dictators!" he yelled. "Megalomaniacs, all of them! They should be here, locked up in an asylum, and you and I should be outside. But they don't consider megalomania a mental disease, do they? I ask you, *Signore* . . ."

He lifted his stick and hit the air angrily with it as if it were a whip which he was lashing at someone he hated. The color in his face deepened and he breathed violently.

Charles stood up. He put his hand gently on the man's shoulder. "Calm yourself," he said. "Calm yourself, Pietro. You are quite right. You are certainly quite right."

"*Molto gentile* . . . you are very kind," Pietro

replied, pulling a large handkerchief out of his pocket and wiping his face with it. "I am suffering from high blood pressure. I should not get excited."

His eyes moved quickly in their sockets, like bird's eyes, or like the pupils of somebody very drunk. Several people were coming through the large portal in their direction.

"Let's walk," said Pietro. "I don't care for their company. You see, *Signore,* I am not really crazy."

"I am not crazy," Charles had told Bruno. "I am not crazy," he had yelled at the doctor. Now this man, Pietro, walking with surprisingly long, swift strides beside him, had said the same thing. "I am not really crazy." And though he had put one more word into the sentence, it had been said with great sincerity, with the well-chosen intonation on the one important word *not,* with the same stress which he, Charles, had tried to put on it, wanting more than anything in the world to convince the listener that he spoke the truth.

"The first thing a crazy person will do is try to convince the one he meets that he is not crazy." Who had said that? Doc Malkiel, once, in a discussion. At that time he had been a young punk of a reporter, writing up a private sanitarium. This man, then, was crazy. But if this man was crazy then he, Charles J. Barrett . . .

"*Caro amico,*" Pietro said, giving him a little poke in the ribs. "Stop thinking. Stop figuring things out. It's no good in a country ruled by a dictator. That's against the law. You can't run around a living example of individuality! They shoot you for that kind of thing!"

He started to chuckle again, his shoulders hunched, and looked for a fleeting second like a vicious little dwarf out of Andersen's fairy tales.

"They'll shoot you and me and the doctor and Bruno and several others," Pietro said, speaking now in a whisper. "You'll see. Just watch, and you'll see. But maybe, this time, we'll shoot first."

He doesn't even know where he is, thought Charles. He doesn't even know that his ideas can't possibly do any more harm, that he is safe behind bars, free to shoot his mouth off. Poor chap. He doesn't know that they have rendered him harmless.

"I came here of my own free will," Pietro told him. "I rather like this place. It's safe. Fairly safe."

Now they had reached the little chapel which, early in the morning, Charles had seen from his window. Standing in front of it, he saw it had one of those delightful multicolored painted façades, on which the last traces of gold on the round haloes of the angles glimmered in the full sunlight.

He didn't know what made him ask the question, curiosity or politeness, or just the urge to keep from thinking. "How long have you been here?"

"Eight months," answered Pietro, counting the names of the past months on his fingers like a child.

They entered the chapel. It was cool.

Pietro went to the basin which held the holy water, and crossed himself. Charles watched his lips move in silent prayer. Then he said aloud, his voice scarcely audible, "I am a good Catholic, and I hate the Germans."

He went on into the very small nave and kneeled down in one of the few pews. The asylum had obviously been built on ground which had once been a private estate, and the chapel had been allowed to remain between the cyprus and oleander hedges as a decoration or as a symbol, because it was much too tiny to hold as many people as the size of the asylum suggested.

Several long and short candles were burning in their simple iron holders under a painting of Saint Francis of Assisi, and a little light flickered in its green storm glass under a painting of the Holy Virgin. It was a little work of art of primitive beauty and though no famous initial could be found on it, it had undoubtedly been painted by a master of the fourteenth century. Charles grew calmer, the longer he looked at it. He couldn't remember when last the atmosphere of a church had touched him. God, to him, was where he found Him, on a mountaintop or in the deep greens of the valley, in the beauty and in the terror of all things, in the moral law of everything.

The man who had chosen to forget his name and who called himself Pietro was kneeling in deep prayer, his forehead resting on his folded hands. At irregular intervals Charles could hear him sigh, the deep sigh of a man who carries too heavy a burden and is tired of it. Peasants sighed that way, quite unconsciously, and therefore without hope. Charles couldn't help feeling embarrassed. Whoever this man was, however poor of spirit and mind, he didn't want to watch him so utterly entranced.

He moved on tiptoe out of the chapel and walked over to the hedge of oleander which was heavy with the first blooms of early spring. Later in the summer, they would flower again, their colors deeper, and then, for a third time, in the autumn. He broke a little twig and held it close to his face. Where would he be then? Would he be condemned to see them blossom again and again?

He moved some strong branches aside. They hid the iron fence which was set on top of the completely bare and even stone walls. To try to get away in daylight would be sheer foolishness. They would catch him right away, and he was quite sure that by evening every patient would have to be in and the portal would be locked. Still, it might be worth trying to make a getaway during the daytime. At least he would have the chance of running into some people and telling them that he wasn't Vittorio da Ponte but Charles J. Barrett. He heard steps behind him on the few uneven flagstones which led up to the chapel and turned quickly.

Pietro was standing there, shaking his head. His face looked rested and there was a slight twinkle in his eye.

"No use," he said. "I've thought of the same thing. It doesn't work. The place is too well guarded." And he broke into a storm of laughter. "*Caro amico,*" he went on, "don't you realize that they are afraid of us, of you and me and of many others? They are scared, I tell you. They are insane with fear that we might break loose and try to put some sense into them!"

From out of nowhere, Bruno suddenly appeared, stood still, clicked his heels and saluted in the military way. "Your Excellency," he said, in a mocking voice. "The *dottore* wants to see you right away, that is, if it suits Your Excellency."

Pietro was obviously angered. He lifted his stick

as he had done once before and fumbled with it. "You dog!" he cried. "You . . . you Judas Iscariot!" And he cursed. "Can't you leave me alone?" And he stamped off violently.

Bruno began to laugh, softly and derisively.

"Why do you get him all upset?" said Charles, suddenly indignant and strangely annoyed. Why should he be interested in a crazy, fifty-year-old man? Why should he resent Bruno's way of treating this Pietro? But there was no denying it. He did.

"Why do you call him 'Excellency'? Why do you tease him?"

"The old fool," said Bruno. "When he came here, he was always trying to impress it on all of us that he was a general, although he never enjoyed higher rank than that of captain. So we call him 'Excellency' just to please him and keep him quiet. But then, again, he has days when he does not want to be reminded of anything that has to do with war. One never knows. He's completely nutty."

"I should like to know what you think of me," said Charles sharply. "What do you tell the other patients about me?"

Bruno yawned. "I never talk to the patients I am not taking care of personally," he replied, and his voice suddenly sounded dignified and almost hurt. "I only talk to the doctor and to my favorite patients and maybe, once in a while, to the other attendants." And now the expression on his face was a mixture of peevishness and pride.

Why, the man's an actor! thought Charles—But maybe all Italians are. . . . It astonished him that Bruno considered him, to quote his own words, "a favorite patient." He hadn't thought so a little while earlier when the same man had twisted his arm around. But maybe he considered things like that just a part of his duties.

"Bruno," he asked, "do you think I am hopeless? I mean, do you think that I could be cured?"

Bruno stared at him hard for a second. "It's just that we can't keep you straight," he answered; "that we can't break you of this silly habit of yours of playing the American. Sometimes you get along beautifully and we think we've done it and then there'll be a relapse like the one you suffered this morning, and you'll insist that you aren't Vittorio da Ponte."

"I don't know what makes me do that," said Charles. "I just wake up feeling as if I didn't know any of you, as if I'd never been here."

"It's the war," Bruno said kindly. "It has happened to many people. They get a shock and then, when they come to, they don't want any more to be the one to whom the awful thing has happened and they invent a story to escape from themselves."

"I'm sorry I've been such a nuisance," said Charles. He was walking back now, following Bruno up the path that led to the house.

"Oh, that's all right. You don't usually give me much trouble. That's because you are a gentleman, Signor Vittorio."

How easy it is to fool people, thought Charles. . . . At that moment Bruno turned and said threateningly, "Now don't you play any tricks. You behave yourself during luncheon. No monkey business!"

"I couldn't have luncheon in my room?"

Bruno shook his head. "No. The *dottore* wants you to meet people again. You always get a sort of craving for loneliness when you pretend to be *il americano,* Signor Barrett. He thinks it's time you got over that."

Charles followed him into the large dining room, where he was shown a place between the man Pietro and a very young man who looked like a student and moved anxiously aside to make room for him to sit down. Misericordia nuns served a poor meal. Pietro told Charles that they had taken over when so many of the male staff had had to be released for war service.

Charles had heard a good deal about the food shortage in Europe, but had never been able to imagine how bad it really was. Now he could see for himself. The portion dealt out to him wouldn't have made a decent breakfast for a six-year-old youngster in the U.S.A.

Attendants guarded them, posted at strategic places here and there behind patients that needed special attention. Charles didn't dare look up and watch the different faces along the table because, the only time he did, he saw the man opposite slobbering his food all over the table, and the attendant, slapping his fingers, showed him how to move the spoon, spilling it over his poor face. Charles felt sick with pity, embarrassment and horror, and he was glad when the meal was over and he could get out.

Pietro stopped him in the hall. "I hope I didn't bother you too much this morning," he said. "The doctor was very angry with me for having annoyed you. Forgive me."

"Please don't feel that way," Charles said. "I . . . I really enjoyed your company."

"You are a true democrat," said Pietro, "a democrat at heart, aren't you? You are kind. Then I will hope to have the pleasure of talking to you again."

"Any time."

"Any time? You mean what you say?"

A man yelling at the top of his lungs and foaming at the mouth was ushered by two attendants past them and into the elevator which Charles noticed now was to the right of the staircase. He turned his face in the other direction quickly.

"*Caro amico,*" Pietro's voice whispered close to his ear. "Why be so sensitive? Haven't you heard people shouting before, foaming at the mouth? And listened to them? Because you listened, you are here now. Don't you understand, *caro amico?*" And, like a child, proud and happy about something it has said or done or experienced, he began to dance, all by himself, holding his stick up in both hands as if it were a partner, smiling the angelic smile of the complete idiot.

Suddenly there was a big commotion outside the door; telephones began ringing all over the house. Dr. Pederazzini and two or three other doctors he hadn't seen before came rushing down the stairs, followed by attendants who started to usher the patients into the elevator and, when that was crammed, started pushing them up the stairs.

"But they were not expected before late afternoon," Charles heard Pederazzini say. "How inconsiderate, just when siesta . . ."

"Quick, quick!" Bruno's hands took hold of Charles's shoulder, pressing him on. "Upstairs. Quick! Out of the way!" And when Charles turned his head to see whether Pietro was still there, dancing crazily and happily, the little *capitano* had gone.

"What is it all about?" he managed to ask Bruno, who seemed in a terrific hurry. But Bruno didn't answer. He didn't even shake his head, just urged him on, till he had him safe in his room.

"Once again – you keep quiet now," he said as a last warning before he left.

Charles went over to the window. He could see a car approach the building, a black car, its horn blowing incessantly, as if to say, "Here I come, make room, quick, make room for a German military official!" But the old trees refused to obey, the path grew smaller and forced the car to a stop.

He watched three men get out of it while a chauffeur and a soldier remained seated, the chauffeur still honking the horn. The other three walked quickly up the path: a German officer, a German sergeant and an Italian lieutenant. If they had come up the back way, they would not have had to stop their car, they would have found ample room to drive up in all their glory . . . but only to the back door of the institution.

In front of the big portal, they stopped. Apparently it had not yet been opened to them. The German officer was furious. "What's this!" he bellowed at his companions. "I am not going to have to wait for these idiots, or am I?"

He turned sharply to the little Italian: "And, of course, I was right in presuming that this building would do excellently for our wounded soldiers. It is ideally located. Why did you try to talk me out of coming here personally? Of course, we shall take over."

The lieutenant answered in a voice thin and high with indignation, "That won't be easy. This is no private sanitarium, *Capitano*. This is a state institution. We will first have to find room for those patients which are here now, before . . ."

The captain tapped his foot impatiently at the same place on the staircase where Charles had stood several hours ago. "You'll never learn, will you?" he said, and the cheap smile of sarcasm was spreading over his face. "What good are these idiots anyhow? With what their maintenance costs, one could do more useful things. We have long ago given up caring for them. We send them to Poland or somewhere where they will die quickly, and others we shoot."

The lieutenant said nothing. He held his head bent, and stared at the point of his shiny black boots.

"Upon my return," said the captain, "I will ask to have this building evacuated. We'll find a way to take care of its present occupants."

Then the door opened noiselessly and they disappeared.

Charles closed the window. He even drew the curtains, quite mechanically. Then he noticed that his hands were trembling. He looked at them. They were sensitive hands, but they were strong, capable hands, too, hands that had worked at tool dressing in the oil fields, that had swung a bat, that had thrown a football, that could handle a rifle and keep a boat on its course.

One less, he thought, one less. . . . It might not be much but it was better than nothing. One less, one man less – one who could not be cruel any more, who could no longer hurt others, who wouldn't ever command less powerful people again – was . . . well, was one man less. There was nothing to stop him from killing this man.

He looked about him for something that could serve as a weapon and only then did he notice that, as on a ship, table, cupboard and chest were fixed to the floor in a way that made it impossible to move them. The only thing that was movable was the small, light chair.

Again he looked at his hands. They were large enough to span a throat, strong enough to press and strangle a man.

And why not? The entire West, of his country, with its simple and straightforward laws, was wide awake in him. Why not? An idiot had attacked the captain . . . a crazy man who didn't know what he was doing. Crazy, he thought, crazy . . . What would be the consequences? They would probably shoot every patient, which was what they were intending to do anyhow . . . just to be rid of them . . .

No. He couldn't do it. Not because he believed that all the mentally ill were not better off dead, but because the thought came to him that among these afflicted men there might be one or two cases where treatment could effect a cure, and because he believed so sincerely in humankind, even if it was crazed, because he had been brought up to respect human life no matter how poor and silly. Because an institution was one of those monuments to civilization, symbolic of the hope man placed in the science he had discovered and developed. No. He couldn't do it, because then disaster would be unavoidable. Now it was only pending. They all still had a chance; the Italians might yet prove stronger.

And then, for the first time since he had seen the car drive up, he thought of himself. Here, perhaps, was the chance he had been looking for – here was someone from the outside world that he had wanted to reach, someone to whom he could walk up and say, "This, my being here, is a case of mistaken identity. I am Charles J. Barrett, American. If you don't believe me, please check with military headquarters, with anyone who handles prisoners of war."

His door was not locked. Bruno, in his vexed hurry, had forgotten to lock it.

The corridor was empty.

As he came to the top of the stairs, he could hear the humming noise of the elevator. He ran down the steps and reached the hall just as they were coming out of it, led by Dr. Pederazzini.

For a second the doctor seemed petrified to find him standing there in front of him. He grew pale. Charles thought he could see his jaw tremble with fury.

"What are you doing here, Signor Vittorio?" he said sharply. "Get out of the way and go up to your room at once."

"Mine is a case of mistaken –" Charles started to say. He felt his heart pounding. It was very difficult to find the words.

"Stop babbling," said the doctor.

He reached out with his hands as if he wanted to push Charles into the now empty elevator, but the captain interrupted him.

"What does this man want?" he said. "Let him speak."

He stepped back but never once took his eyes off Charles's face. He stared at him with the rudeness and impertinent arrogance no member of any other race was ever able to express. What he was after, apparently, was to humiliate the little Italian lieutenant by proving the point he had made before with this Italian idiot as an example.

Charles spoke quickly, the words tumbling from his mouth. "I am an American, I am a prisoner of war, this is a horrible mistake . . . a case of mistaken identity." He hadn't meant to say it because he knew now how wrong it was and what kind of reaction it would create, but he said it just the same — "I am not crazy. Believe me, I am not crazy!"

Whereupon they all began to laugh aloud, the captain loudest of them all. He laughed so hard, it sounded like a pony neighing. "*Non sono idiota,*" he repeated, mocking the lieutenant. "*Non sono idiota. Crede . . .*"

In a way, his face was quite handsome, wide blue eyes, long lashes, apple-red cheeks and a thin, long mouth, except for the fact that he had practically no chin. It must have stopped growing when he was still a nasty little boy of eleven, writing dirty jokes on walls, leaving drawings on the seats of toilets. . . .

The sergeant laughed because his captain laughed, and the doctor laughed, too. Only the little lieutenant didn't laugh.

"*Non sono idiota . . .*" Why, he had spoken

Italian! Introducing himself dramatically as an American, a prisoner of war, he had not spoken English, but Italian! The moment he opened his lips to correct this mistake, someone (later he discovered it had been Bruno) lifted him from behind as if he – five feet, nine-and-a-half inches tall, weighing one hundred and sixty-five pounds – were a child. When he came to, Bruno was standing in front of him.

"You idiot!" he said. "You idiot!"

"Have they gone?"

"Two hours ago. I am sorry I had to knock you out. You certainly gave me a lot of trouble. You certainly didn't keep your promise. I should teach you, so that you don't try it again; I really should put you under . . ."

He interrupted himself, controlled now. "I am sorry I had to knock you out," he repeated. This time, after he had left the room, he locked the door.

Charles lay very quiet after he had gone. He was worn out. Never before, or so it seemed to him, had so many different emotions raced through his heart and brain. Bewilderment, frantic bewilderment, fury, and deep embarrassment. Now he couldn't feel anything any more. He was tired of everything, desperately tired. He lay, his arms folded behind his head on the hard little cushion, and watched the dusk settle before his window with the sudden wild change of light he had once admired so much. For the first time in his life he experienced hopelessness to its very depths. He tried to follow this thought, hanging onto it as if he were afraid he might otherwise fall into a vacuum. He had never been without hope before. Exhausted, blue, scared, desperate – yes. But there had always been something worth trying again, a possibility calling for use of brain and body. Now there was nothing. Nothing. With eyes wide open, unblinking, he stared into the soft darkness of early evening.

He hadn't been brought up to give in. Not he, born and raised by American parents in the wild open spaces of the West. He had been brought up amid the big dreams that helped people build their country, in the firm belief that any man with good horse sense and an able body had a chance to form the life he wanted to live. And though this conviction had had to weather many storms and had sometimes been badly shaken up, he still believed in opportunity and individualism.

Bruno came in and asked him to come downstairs to eat. He shook his head. He wasn't hungry. After a while, another attendant came and brought him a plate of *minestrone* and a bowl of *risotto*. Charles didn't touch it.

His thoughts wandered. He recalled prisoners who had gone on a hunger strike to force an issue. But here, where he was confined, they would only consider it another crazy fit and probably feed him forcibly.

Then the doctor put in an appearance. "*Buona sera,* Signor Vittorio. I hear you feel very depressed." He sat down at the foot of the bed. Charles didn't answer.

"Pull yourself together," Pederazzini said. "You mustn't let yourself go, *Signore!* It doesn't do any good." His voice was mild and kind.

Charles, who had expected to be reproached for the scene he had created in the lobby, looked up in surprise. Nothing made sense any more. Whatever he did seemed to have the reverse reaction from the one he expected.

"Why don't you give in?" said the doctor. "Why do you fight so hard against reality? Why don't you want to be what you are? Why do you want to be Charles Barrett? Charles Barrett is dead. He died twenty-four years ago, in 1918. He tried to escape from a German prison train and was shot to death when he wouldn't obey the guard's order to halt. You see? He's dead."

"Yes," said Charles. "He's dead."

"You should remember that," said the doctor. "Whenever you don't like to be Vittorio da Ponte, and want to escape from his personality and become someone else, you should remember that you can't become Charles Barrett. Because Charles Barrett is dead."

"Maybe you're right."

"Of course, I'm right," the doctor went on cheerfully. "If you would just always remember . . ." He got up. "You shouldn't lie here in the dark, all alone. It's not time to sleep yet, and if you rest your body now, you won't have a good night."

"Thank you," said Charles.

"Why don't you go and see Pietro?" the doctor suggested. "He seems to like you . . . you seem to be able to calm him. He was very upset by our visitors this afternoon. If it isn't troubling you too much, why don't you go over and talk to him for a while before retiring? His room is just opposite yours. *Buona notte,* Signor Vittorio."

"*Buona notte, Dottore.*"

He listened for the key to be turned in the door, but it wasn't. He could hear the doctor's steps grow gradually fainter. Pederazzini was right. He shouldn't lie here, he shouldn't give up. He should pull himself together.

He got up and washed his face and neck and his hands, and a little while later he knocked at the door opposite his own.

"Come in," he could hear Pietro call out, "come in." He pressed the handle down.

The room was not very different from the one he had found himself in on awakening. Yet it had a certain atmosphere which contrasted strangely with the sober white walls and furniture. Pietro remained seated in front of his desk when Charles entered. He was pushing aside a heap of papers. About two dozen sharply pointed pencils lay in neat order in front of him. One of them was sticking behind his large right ear, apparently forgotten.

"I didn't mean to disturb you," said Charles.

"Not at all, not at all," said Pietro. "I am just clearing up. I hope you don't mind." He was sorting sheet after sheet, covered with the tiny light letters of his handwriting.

"You see, *amico mio,*" he said, "I am writing my biography." He smiled vaguely. "Nice reading it will make someday. Let's hope humankind will learn something from it. Do you think they will? I don't, actually. I'm just doing it for the sake of science . . . a sort of legacy to science, let's say."

"I didn't know you were a colleague of mine," said Charles, and sat down opposite the small desk. "I am a writer, or, let's say, I was a writer. A playwright."

"I am no writer. I am a general," said Pietro. He leaned back and his left hand tapped the desk. "Quite a good general at that. A good strategist, I might say. Except that I don't believe in wars. Never have. Not in the first World War, not in the Abyssinian war, not in this one."

He laughed.

Charles took his eyes off Pietro's face. . . . There he goes, he thought. He could hear Bruno's mocking voice: "When he came here, he was always trying to impress it on all of us that he was a general although he never enjoyed higher rank than that of captain."

"We are funny people," Pietro said, and now he got up and began to pace the room, his arms crossed behind his back. "Whether we are loyal to the King or loyal to our country or playing along with the Fascists or have communistic tendencies – there is always one thing that unites us all, and that is our hatred of the Germans. Barbarians!" And he raised his voice.

"They destroyed us once, in ancient times. Because of them we fought the last war and had to take its consequences. And now, again." He paused, stood still for a moment, leaning against the wall. Then he went on. "We don't hate France and we don't hate England and we don't hate

America, but we do hate the Germans. Ah . . ." he said thoughtfully, and stroked his thin, gray hair.

"We are patriots. Maybe not in the sense you understand it, yet we are patriots. District patriots. Every Italian loves the district he was born in, and will do anything to prevent it being harmed or destroyed. Maybe that is real patriotism. I don't know."

He stared into the open palms of his hands, holding them spread out in front of him. "The Germans . . . If we don't stop them, they will ruin us. Why don't you help me stop them, *amico mio?*"

Charles grinned with embarrassment and fury. He had volunteered to help stop the Germans and had ended in a lunatic asylum, listening to a crazy little *capitano* who thought he was a general, who thought he could change the fate of his country from behind bars.

"*Allora!*" said Pietro. "Why don't you do something?"

"Well, I did try – my way!" said Charles.

Pietro snorted like a horse, his face showing contempt, almost disgust. "And who is stopping you now?"

Charles shrugged his shoulders. What was he supposed to say to that?

"You don't see it, do you?" Pietro asked.

"Sorry. No."

Again Pietro began to laugh and, laughing, slapped his thigh.

"Well," he said, "I see it. I see it very clearly."

"If I ever did get a chance to stick my face out of here, I'd be imprisoned right away."

"How stupid you are! *Stupido! Stupido!*" exclaimed Pietro. "And I always thought Americans were so bright. But perhaps you are no American, after all. Maybe you . . . And you haven't any guts, have you? You don't want to take any risks, do you? You don't want to help the Americans to finish the war a little quicker and avoid more bloodshed, do you? Oh, I am so disappointed."

"I'd certainly like to know what's on your mind," said Charles. He didn't know why he felt insulted by a little man who was obviously nuts. "Why don't you go ahead and tell me?"

"Why should I tell you, if you don't want to cooperate, eh? Why should I?"

He looked at Charles, his eyes dancing with excitement. "If I tell you . . . you would have to promise me one thing . . ."

Charles began to laugh.

"All right, all right," he said. "Go ahead. Shoot. I promise anything you want me to." Maybe, in his cracked mind, the little *capitano* had an idea that might help his mind onto the right track. Nothing was too fantastic if it promised a chance of real escape.

"You know the Contessa San Vigilio, don't you?"

Pietro now sat down opposite Charles again. The pencil was still sticking behind his ear.

Charles shook his head.

"But . . . I thought you had been in Rome?"

"I know Rome, but I didn't mix with the aristocracy."

"She was American, originally. Everyone knows Luisa San Vigilio. She is a very clever woman, a good woman, a good American, and she loves my country."

Luisa San Vigilio. Naturally. He knew the name. When had he seen her last? In 1937. She had been about forty, then, a tall, beautifully groomed woman, one of those American women who so greatly influenced the development of Italian womanhood, not only through their mentality, but through their whole way of life. Italian women, and especially the women of Rome, had always been lovely, but American blood had made them truly beautiful. It had added to their exciting teeth and the rich quality of their hair and the depth of their eyes, the long straight legs and the easy grace of the Anglo-Saxon. And once their bodies had been thus transformed by this healthy, foreign blood, the Italian women had wanted to use their straighter, slender limbs, had begun to interest themselves in sports, something almost unknown to them before. Those American women who had married into the Italian aristocracy — which, in this country, would always lead the way — had refused to live the dependent, quiet life of the average Italian woman. They had clung to their independence, and soon the others had begun to imitate them, had even dared to go out alone, had dared to be seen alone on the streets, something unheard of before — when, if a family couldn't afford a dignified chaperone, they would at least find a maid, even if she were only a little twelve-year-old child, to see the young *signorina* to college, or to accompany her to her game of tennis or on a shopping expedition.

Pietro was saying, "You must go and see her. Go and tell her Pietro sent you . . . just — Pietro."

"I will."

He had never felt so close to tears as now, watching the excited features of the little *capitano* with whom he was playing this silly game — out of friendship, or just because he hadn't the heart to get up and say to the old chap, "Leave me alone, will you?"

"There are people here," Pietro went on, "people with power and of high rank, who would like to help the Americans, help them to land when, sooner or later, they will have to invade my country. I haven't the list with all the names . . . maybe nobody has a list . . . but one man knows them all, and to this man Luisa San Vigilio will take you. Her house is well known. She lives near the Pincio. You will memorize that list — you will, *caro amico*, and you will somehow get it to the Americans. Promise?"

"Promise," said Charles.

Pietro stretched out his hand. "Give me your hand, *carissimo*. Let me shake you by the hand, *amico mio*. Let me thank you most sincerely in the name of my country."

And he was crying now, the big tears running down his cheeks, his jaw moving.

Charles looked away. He felt his fingers almost crushed in the surprisingly strong grip of the little man who held them as though locked in a medieval torture instrument.

After a little while, when Pietro had regained his composure, Charles withdrew his hand. "Well," he said, getting up.

"Wait," said Pietro. "I haven't told you yet where your chance lies. Or do you know now? Have you thought of it?" A smile spread across his face. "It just happens that *I'm* so foolish as to believe your story, to believe that you are an American. You see, as an American you wouldn't have a chance of escape. But . . ."

The world seemed to tumble. Suddenly, Charles knew!

"But as Vittorio da Ponte I have all the chance in the world!" he said slowly, and sat down again.

For a moment he remained silent. As Vittorio da Ponte he had all the chance in the world. Of course! Vittorio da Ponte, born in Verona in the year 1900. He had a father, Francesco da Ponte, who came from Venice and had red hair, and had been killed in battle on the Col di Lana. . . . The injection Bruno had given must have been pretty strong to have kept his mind so dulled that he had not thought of this obvious way out!

Suddenly he found himself breathing heavily with excitement. Be Vittorio da Ponte? Escape as Vittorio da Ponte? But what was the use of that? They would send out an alarm and bring him right back.

What had the doctor said that morning? Something about his having been so much better in the last two years that he had almost thought of releasing him as cured, that this was the first bad relapse he had suffered for months. . . .

Release, thought Charles. If I could have an official release from Pederazzini, if I could have papers proving that I, Vittorio da Ponte, have been confined for almost twenty-five years in this asylum and am now being released as perfectly harmless. If . . . if I could obtain those papers . . . I could walk through all of Italy and somehow make my way into Switzerland and get in touch from there with . . ."

But would Pederazzini give him a release, now, after the scene he had made this afternoon? Pederazzini would have to be convinced that he was cured of Charles Barrett.

Or . . .

He suddenly remembered the talk he had overheard when the German captain had arrived — the talk about evacuating the asylum. Undoubtedly he had spoken to Pederazzini about that, too. Perhaps the mad idea would never be realized, perhaps, for once, the Italians wouldn't bow to orders; but perhaps Pederazzini would be more willing to release him on account of the danger which threatened the asylum.

When he finally looked up, he saw that Pietro had fallen asleep, his body sagging in the chair, his face lying on the little pile of paper. He was snoring heavily. . . . Poor devil, thought Charles. He'll probably never know how deeply grateful I am to him for being crazy enough to have led me to a brilliant idea.

CHAPTER III

VITTORIO DA PONTE stood in the small, narrow, crowded corridor of the train, racing through the Campagna in the direction of Rome. Here and there in the wide, flat landscape, between high cypresses and low olive trees, he could see the round mounds of the old Roman graves which, according to an old legend, were the burial places of the heroes of the battles between Horatians and the Curiatians. Once, long ago, an enthusiastic young scholar named Charles J. Barrett had walked on foot through the same landscape, a knapsack on his shoulders and a stick in his right hand, looking about him with enchanted eyes, his heart beating with satisfaction. Rome . . . One of his dreams had come true. But that Charles J. Barrett from Tulsa, Oklahoma, was dead.

A smile fluttered across Vittorio's face.

How easy it had been in the end! So much easier than he ever would have expected. Dr. Pederazzini himself had made the first move, a day after

Charles's visit to Pietro's room. "If I could only trust you," he had said, "I would release you. At any time now, we may have to find another place for you which might not be at all to your advantage. If you could just pull yourself together and decide to be yourself, I would like to send you home, to Verona, to your own house. It's your house, you know. Your mother left it to you when she died, and it has been well taken care of ever since. But first I would advise you to go to Rome. It is easier to get a permit to travel there, and you might like to see the city. Though you are not wealthy, you are quite well off – I mean, you will have enough for a decent, quiet life. You should keep very quiet."

Charles Barrett had sat very still. He understood very well what the doctor was trying to do – to save those people who, he felt, couldn't do any harm, from a dreadful fate. He had looked at Pederazzini, and had seen how pale and worn out the doctor's face was. This man, seated opposite him, had obviously not slept since he had last seen him. For a moment he had tried to imagine himself in the other man's place, faced with such terrible responsibility, which he alone had to bear with all its consequences and blame, wondering how far he could go in his effort to rescue his patients from being shot or sent into frightful exile, taking the worst for granted – by experience and by temperament.

"In your case I feel justified in releasing you," Pederazzini had said, "though I would have preferred to have you with us till I could be absolutely sure of you. Yet, when I come to think of it, there are many more crazy people outside this building, people that do more harm than any one of you could do, murdering . . . Well, anyhow, I shall let you go."

And today he had been released.

He had not seen Pietro again because his strange and violent behavior the night after Charles had left him had made it necessary for him to be kept in a padded cell.

Vittorio da Ponte felt for the wallet in his hip-pocket. He was carrying all sorts of papers which had been handed to him on leaving, a document from the Casa della Pace, with a seal and three signatures, a birth certificate, some of the photos he had found in the drawer of his desk and a roll of money.

It was the money which had startled him more than anything else and which had aroused suspicion in him for the first time since all his frustrated efforts to prove that he was Charles J. Barrett had begun. For the first time he had begun to think that the reason for his release might not be mere decency on the part of the doctor, whose sense of fairness had been aroused by the very brutality of the Germans and their plan to send his patients into horrible exile or have them shot to get rid of them. For the first time he had begun to think that there might be something more to it.

Why had he been sent to a lunatic asylum instead of to a prison camp? Someone had obviously slipped up. But had that someone made the mistake on purpose? Maybe. Maybe not.

And he had looked at the doctor again. Pederazzini was not a stupid man. His eyes were much too intelligent for that. He couldn't really believe that he, Charles J. Barrett, was Vittorio da Ponte. He couldn't. He *knew* he wasn't. Why, then, did the doctor insist that he was da Ponte?

And then, all of a sudden, he had known why.

And now, standing in the crowded train, he was sure he was right.

Someone had made a mistake, whether on purpose or not he probably would never know, and had sent him to the Casa della Pace instead of to a prison camp, and the doctor had found out that he was an American and had decided to help him to escape . . . Him, the American. Why? Maybe just because Pederazzini hated the Germans, as Pietro did, as all the Italians did. Or maybe the doctor had once been in love with an American girl or had a brother in America, living somewhere, maybe in Brooklyn, or there might be some other bond. . . . He, Charles, would never know.

And Pederazzini, with the slyness of a diplomat, had decided not to tell him, hadn't said to him, "I know who you are. You were brought here by mistake. I want to help you to escape," but had preferred to cover himself in every conceivable way, even from the man he was saving; had preferred, instead of saying, "Vittorio da Ponte died here. It happened that he died shortly before you arrived. We will bury him as Charles J. Barrett and you will take his name and his papers because this is the only chance of escape you have"; had preferred not to take any risk at all, in case Charles J. Barrett were caught and his identity found out.

That was it. Of course. He could think of no other explanation. Not now. Not yet.

Through the window he could see the old Via Appia, and, now, the golf links opposite the modern airfield where, years ago, he had played his eighteen holes in the company of foreign journalists and a few Italian girls who had been extraordinarily good at it. Here and there one would find a snake wriggling across the soft greens or lying rolled into a little round black heap on the soft warm sand of the bunkers. The pro would always deny that there were snakes around the links, so once they had played a dirty trick on him and had placed a small garter snake in his locker just to convince him. How childish and carefree those days had been! His first spring in Rome: the horse show at the Villa Borghese where, before a brilliant audience, the Italian team always won the first prizes. . . . Jackie Loft from United Press had insisted that here they had their only chance because they had schooled their horses over the course, in the middle of the night, so that next day horse and rider were acquainted with every obstacle. But that had been pure jealousy, because his girl, Cleme, had fallen head over heels in love with one of the Italian officers, the one to whom she had presented the large silver cup. . . . Ah, and those first warm nights, when one could drive out along the old Via Appia and find a little place, among the tall marguerites that were almost as big as little sunflowers, which the girls picked by the bushel or wound into wreaths; and the men brought along chianti, or sweet, sparkling asti, the Italian version of champagne; and one could lie among the tall flowers, white in the light of a full moon which rode the sky and lighted up the white marble of the big round tower of the mausoleum of Cecilia Metella. Somewhere near the sepulcher, someone would be playing a guitar, and the dark voice of a man or the sweet, high soprano of a girl would ring through the night, singing one of the sentimental little folksongs so typical of the natives of this country, whose indifference to all the events of life as long as they didn't hurt the one and only important thing – the family – had led them to accept dictatorship, and had finally, and so logically, led them into war . . . on the side of the Germans whom they hated. . . .

Pietro . . . he thought. Pietro was right. He hadn't lost his mind to such an extent that he couldn't remember this cardinal fact: the centuries-old hatred of the Barbarian.

Now, in a little while, the train would reach its destination, the Termini Station. He drew a deep breath. As he stood in the crowded, badly smelling corridor, its floor covered with discarded newspapers and the remains of food – no cigaret stubs, though – his back against the small closed door of the compartment, the last few days seemed like a nightmare, too fantastic to be believed in these everyday surroundings of people chatting, trying to elbow their way through to another car, wheels singing on the shiny tracks, a little boy whistling, a little girl whispering in her mother's ear that she had to go to the toilet and just couldn't hold it till they got to Rome, German and Italian soldiers in strict segregation, playing cards . . . too fantastic to be believed. Things like that didn't happen. A prisoner of war, finding himself in a lunatic asylum instead of in a camp, an ordinary guy turned into a Vittorio da Ponte, taking over another man's personality just like that – a man who might be dead or alive for all he knew – as the only way of escape, resigning himself to the fact of having been crazy and in confinement for almost twenty-five years! It couldn't be true! He must have dreamed it!

He looked down at his legs, dressed in trousers he had never seen before. His hand searched for the wallet . . . there were the initials, V.dP. He put it back into his hip-pocket. All of a sudden, with the realization of what he had escaped, he shuddered. What if Dr. Pederazzini had been a Fascist and perverted enough to keep him at the asylum instead of turning him over to military officials?

The train thundered into the station, slowed down, came to a stop, its wheels screeching. He bent to pick up his two large suitcases and stood in a line that moved surprisingly slowly. When it was his turn to step down, he understood why. At the doors of every car, guards were posted, military police, as well as the *milizia.* A harsh voice asked the routine question, "*Carta d'identità?*"

And only then, when expert eyes began comparing his papers and photograph – the one that had been taken an hour before he had been released, in the doctor's office, and had been pasted on the empty place designed for it – with himself, did Charles J. Barrett fully realize what his situation was: that of an American, an enemy, trying to make his way through a country with which his own was at war.

"*Casa della Pace, davvero?*" said the man, giving him a scrutinizing look. "*Ecco!*"

Charles took the papers and folded them back into his wallet. His hands were shaking. . . . I mustn't tremble, he thought. I must not tremble. I have nothing to be afraid of. I am here with legitimate papers, I am an Italian, I am Vittorio da Ponte who has been in confinement for twenty-four years. . . . In the confusion and bewilderment of the last few days, it had somehow not yet occurred to him that he would have to use all his energy and concentration to deceive the people around him, to fool them and all the military officials and all the different officials of the German and Italian police, to make them believe that he was actually what his papers said he was – Vittorio da Ponte; that never, not even for a second, could he let himself think of Charles Barrett; that he would have to concentrate on being da Ponte, on his language; that he could not slip up, even once! . . . "Don't open your mouth too much when you speak, Charley," he told himself. "Let it come out sort of slurred and very soft . . ." He would have to watch his words, his accent, his intonation, his gestures, his face – all the time!

"Move," said the man now, harshly, because Charles was holding up the line. "Get going. There's a war on." And then, remembering the doctor's certificate, "Well, you wouldn't know. How could you, poor fellow? You'll find yourself in a different world!" And it occurred to him while Charles got lost in the crowd that, after all, the world wasn't so different now from the world this man had left – 1918 . . . Bad luck, thought the little guard. He hadn't had much of life, had he, this fellow? To him it must seem that wars never end, coming back from one straight into another, as if wars were going to go on endlessly. Well, maybe they were. . . .

Charles walked through the station, watching the people, looking at the many posters in Italian and German that plastered the walls, giving exact descriptions of everything. There seemed to be more Germans than Italians.

I must make a plan, he told himself. And I had better get out of this guarded *stazione* quickly.

He was stopped at the entrance to the building and again had to show his papers.

"Where to? What address?"

" . . . I . . ." he stuttered, thinking: I can be shy and slow of words. After all, look where I'm coming *from!*

"If you don't know where you're going, we'd better keep you here. There's not a room to be had anywhere in town. We'd better send you back."

So it was true. They were preventing people from entering Rome, the only city not being bombed, to which people were streaming from all over the country. . . .

"I . . ." said Charles slowly, "I am being expected."

"Where? Address, please."

He thought of giving the address of the little *albergtto,* a small family pension, where he had stayed before, but they would check up on him, and go there he certainly could not – plump Signora Maria would recognize her *americano* right away.

"You'd better step aside and wait," said the *carabiniere.*

Charles said, "The Contessa San Vigilio is expecting me."

"San Vigilio, eh?" said the man, and wet his pencil on the tip of his tongue. "What was your name again? Da Ponte, Vittorio. Coming from where?"

He started to put down all this on a printed

form. Charles groped for his papers; the man glanced over them quickly.

"Casa della Pace. Well, I think they should have kept you there. Staying at the Vigilios'. *Ecco*. Move on," and he gave an impatient little shrug with his shoulders.

Charles walked a few steps until he came to the big Piazza of L'Esedra di Termini, right next to the Terme Diocleziani. There were no taxis, only cars with their military identifications and a few lorries. Some very shabby cabs, their horses old and gaunt from insufficient fodder and too much work, stood along the curb. In the middle of the square, a tall fountain threw its water across several bronze sea goddesses. . . . Where to? thought Charles.

The question was, rather, where not to? He tried to remember all the places where he had been known and therefore could not go. But would the owners of restaurants or hotels recognize him? After all, in the six years since he had last been in Rome, he had changed, most decidedly. Six years lived in the twentieth century would leave their trace on any man. And then, they would never dream of finding among them an American, a member of the nation with whom they were at war although they had never quite believed in that possibility.

He could take the risk. After all, he had only been in Rome four months altogether, and in this city which was visited by so many different nationalities at all times, they wouldn't remember one face so clearly.

He would have liked to look around to find out when and where he could get a room, but he didn't want to go back into the station and leave his baggage there.

He looked back over his shoulder and saw the *carabiniere* standing where he had left him. And it seemed to him as if the man, so busily interviewing people, was watching him out of the corner of one eye.

He hailed one of the shabby cabs and quickly got in.

"Where to?"

Where had Elisa stayed during her three weeks in Rome? Elisa, the young Swiss student from Zürich who could always find places that were clean and proper . . . Somewhere near the Via Vittorio Veneto, where the foreign visitors lived, close to the magnificent old Baroque staircase at the foot of the church of Santissima Trinita dei Monti, which led to the Piazza di Spagna. There Elisa had bought flowers from the open stands which had their place on one of the lower, broader stairs, giving to the lovely gracious lines of this architectural miracle all the color needed to make it absolutely perfect.

Villa Maria? Villa Augusta? How difficult it was to think back across a span of six years . . .

"Via Ludovisi – Villa Elvira."

The cabby clicked his tongue, making a noise as if his mouth were a small pistol from which a shot had been fired, and the horse started to move, dragging the cab behind it, around the square and past the large *ristorante* whose open spaces were crowded with soldiers of both warring nations having their lunch. Charles looked back once to catch a last glimpse of the ruins of the most impressive Thermae which the Romans had ever built. Above them he could see the tower of the church of Santa Maria degli Angeli. Somewhere to the left must be the museum which housed, in a room all by itself, the beautiful torso of the Venus of Kythere.

When they drove up through the Via Vittorio Veneto, Charles noticed for the first time how poor and shabby the people looked, people who had once been among the most elegantly groomed men and women he had ever seen. . . . That's what the war's done, he thought. During his short ride on the train he had not been aware of the poverty, but then most of the passengers had been in uniform.

The cabby stopped in front of a small three-story house where a sign said "VILLA ELVIRA, PENSIONE. *English spoken. On parle français. Man spricht Deutsch.*" "*English spoken*" had been crossed out by two heavy black strokes but "*On parle français*" had not been touched.

Inside there was a small vestibule with several cane chairs and tables, with faded cushions and chintz curtains that had lost their shiny gloss in all too many washings and looked drab. There were two or three traditional palms in modern Majolica jars, apparently to brighten up the room and lend it an atmosphere more Italian. Men used to throw their cigaret stubs into them, not bothering to find the ash trays of which there seemed always to be too few about, and once in a while a child had poured its loathed medicine into their earth. Still, the palms had survived. Under the bend of the stairs stood a small desk with a case for mail and a clock whose hands stood still.

Charles tipped the cabby who had carried the bags into the house and now stood there, clicking his tongue again to get some attention and finally, when no one showed up, volunteering the following information, at the top of his lungs: "The Swiss lady who ran this place has left. Lucky devil, eh, Anna?"

Anna, a plump and very sloppy-looking maid,

poked her head over the bannisters. "*La padrona* isn't here," she said. "We are just serving lunch."

The cabby shrugged his shoulders but seemed to think it his duty to remain until, after a little while, the owner of the pension appeared, obviously bad-tempered at having been disturbed.

"We have no room," she said.

"Even a little one would do," said Charles.

La padrona let her eyes wander over him from top to toe, then she gave the two suitcases a scrutinizing look.

"How long does the *Signore* think of staying?"

Her voice was low and quite melodious, in spite of her sullen face. Charles reached into his pocket, took out the big bundle of notes and began to move his fingers through them.

"Oh, maybe just a while. Perhaps all through the summer."

"One of my tenants fell ill and had to be taken to a hospital. It's a very small room, if the *Signore* cares to see it."

The cabby left, and Charles followed the woman into an elevator which took them to the third floor. The woman, Signora Vertelli, was a rather small and sad-looking creature. "Times are terrible," she told him. "My son was killed in the battle of Crete and my husband is working in a factory. I am sorry, but you can't expect good service."

She opened one of the three doors at the end of a dark little corridor. The room was very small with almost no furniture except for the absolutely essential pieces, but there was a skylight instead of a window, through which one could see the clouds sailing across a blue sky.

"We have no running water in this room, but there is a bathroom. You'll have to share it with two tenants next door."

"This will do," said Charles, and put the baggage, which he had carried up himself, on the floor. "How much is it?"

She named a price which was ridiculously high, and he looked at her in surprise. Her face at once grew sullen again and she shrugged her shoulders. "What do you expect, *Signore?* I have to feed you, don't I? And I can't always get food the regular way."

"It's all right," he said.

She reached into her pocket and handed him a fountain pen and some forms. "Please fill them out at once," she said. "We have to send them over to the *questura* within an hour after a guest arrives or leaves."

Vittorio da Ponte. *Born:* April 13th, 1900, Verona. *Name of the father:* Francesco. *Name of the mother:* Caterina. *Name of brothers and sisters:* None. *Last place of residence: . . .* He hesitated for a moment, then wrote quickly: Verona. *Name of next of kin:* None living. *Otherwise closest relative or friend:* Dr. Pederazzini.

Signora Vertelli was looking over his shoulder. "*Va bene,*" she said.

He watched her leave the room and heard the door click to behind her, the small sighing noise as she started the elevator. He sank into the one and only chair, all of a sudden desperately tired. . . . No, he thought. It's all too easy. Much too easy. Why have I been provided with all these things? That name? Why? . . . Don't start thinking now, he told himself then. You have come to one good conclusion. Let it go at that. Don't bother about it any longer. Pederazzini just wanted to help you to escape once he found out you were an American. Never mind his reasons. Accept the whole thing. Stop trying to figure things out. . . . But his mind would go on working and he couldn't stop it.

All right, he told himself. Then think logically. You figured out one possibility, the obvious one, that somebody made a mistake. Now start from the other angle. Someone didn't make a mistake. Where does that get you? To the point where you, Charles J. Barrett from Tulsa, Oklahoma, were sent to a lunatic asylum on purpose. But why? Why? Who could be interested in having an American running around loose in Italy, which is at war with the United States? The Germans? The Italians?

He buried his face in both hands and could feel his palms perspiring. As a little boy, trying to find a solution to some mathematical problem, he had often sat like this, his head buried in his hands, to shut out everything which might interfere with concentration. There was a wall somewhere which brought his thoughts to a stop with a bang, threw him back on himself like a boomerang. They provided you with a name, with papers, with money. Why?

"They" – never mind who they are – why did they? What was their purpose? Certainly not to make it easier for me to escape or they would have presented me with a travel permit to Verona. But they didn't. They sent me to Rome. They want me in Rome. If it weren't something secret, they wouldn't have sent me to a lunatic asylum, they wouldn't have made such a damn silly mystery of the whole thing, would they? They would have talked to me, saying, "Charles Barrett, we want you to do this and this special thing and we are going to treat you nicely accordingly. If you refuse, we'll shoot you." That's the way they would have behaved if they had wanted me to do something. But they don't want anything of me. I am being used by them for a purpose. . . . What is it?

Oh, damn it all! I'm a simple straightforward American who wasn't brought up to figure out mysteries. I'm a lieutenant in the American Army, ready to be killed if necessary. I didn't go to war to become Vittorio da Ponte. Why am I supposed to be Italian? Why?

To meet some other Italians? But I don't know any important Italians.

I am being used for a certain purpose. A trap, maybe. For someone. But for whom?

He stood up. He began to walk the room, biting his lip. . . . I am an obscure playwright who wants to write a smash hit. I have no other ambition except to do my duty by my country and have a little success for myself . . . I . . . I . . . Where was I?

I am here on purpose. It was no mistake. Mistakes of that kind don't happen. . . . Yes, millions of mistakes happen, fantastic mistakes, especially in wartime. Let's start again . . .

This all happened by intention. The Italians want me here, so they send me to a lunatic asylum. The doctor there knows who I am, he has been notified, he pretends to have known me for twenty-four years, he is not a decent human being, he is a Fascist playing along with those gangsters, so he begins by confusing me, lets me think he does it to cover himself in case I should be caught, lets me think he's out to help me and therefore provides me with all the necessary papers and evidence. . . . Jiminy cricket! They can't think Americans are that stupid! They must have figured on the obvious thing — that I wouldn't believe that I was suffering from amnesia, that I was Vittorio da Ponte. . . . They counted on the fact that I'd wonder. . . . Sure! That's why they led me to believe that Pederazzini is pro-Ally. . . . They send me to Rome. . . . They give me money. . . .

"*San Vigilio, eh?*" The voice of the *carabiniere* who had asked him at which address he would stay rang suddenly in Charles's ear. He stopped dead.

San Vigilio . . . Luisa San Vigilio . . . Born American . . . Married to an Italian count . . . Are they setting a trap for her?

Wait a minute, buddy! Wait a minute. . . . Born American . . . Big social part she's playing — always has — God knows how important her husband is. They send me there as Vittorio da Ponte. Maybe she has known my mother. How do I know with whom my parents mixed? I trust her . . . I tell her . . . I tell her that I am not Vittorio da Ponte, that I, too, am American, that I'm Charles J. Barrett from Tulsa, Oklahoma. . . . And then what?

Then they'd know how she behaves, how she behaves when an American comes to her, a parachutist, an escaped prisoner, a . . . a messenger of some kind. They'd know on whose side she is, on the Americans' or theirs! What she'd do – help him, hide him, give away secrets. . . . And then they could imprison her – shoot her – get rid of the Conte San Vigilio, maybe some other people, too!

That was it! That was it!

They are afraid of an American invasion. They want to find out who is with them and who is against them.

"San Vigilio, eh?" It had been said in such a particular tone, and the *carabiniere* had gone on watching him for such a long time. But maybe he was imagining all this. Was he? Certainly he was.

He sat down, desperate with mental exhaustion. Something was missing. Somewhere he'd made a mistake. The mistake was . . . Dr. Pederazzini had not mentioned the name of the Contessa San Vigilio. The man who had mentioned that name had been the crazy little *capitano,* Pietro.

Charles began to laugh, to laugh to himself. He was going nuts, sitting here, imagining things.

The *capitano* had been crazy and he, Charles, was all wrong. Pederazzini had never mentioned the name, not once, and he would most certainly have done so if he had been playing the part of the Fascist intriguer which Charles had just assigned him. Assignment withdrawn.

What I am doing is just trying to complicate things, he thought. I am building things up because I can't understand the whole thing; and because I can't make head or tail of it, my imagination runs wild. Why? Just because I can't believe in mistakes like this.

Gosh, he thought again, what a beautiful play this would make! The guy who wants the Star-Spangled Banner to fly proudly and secure, getting caught up in European politics; the boy from the West playing a part in international intrigue . . .

There was a knock at the door, and Signora Vertelli came in carrying a tray.

"Lunch has already been served," she told him, "but I thought I would make an exception, just today."

She watched him eat the tiny piece of meat and the rice. "Let me have your ration card," she said. "There are always long queues at the shops. It saves time."

He thought rapidly. He must not make himself conspicuous. He took out his wallet and began to search rapidly through its different little pockets in which he knew there was no ration card.

"*Diavolo!*" he exclaimed. "I've lost it!"

"Lost it?" The woman seemed terrified.

Charles sprang to his feet and began to search frantically in all pockets. "It must have been stolen," he said. "I know, now, I put it in my hip-pocket."

"Will man never learn to watch out?" she cried, helping him to look, reaching into his pockets. "Stolen! Naturally! One doesn't carry one's ration card in one's hip-pocket. You'll have a fine time getting a new one issued. To fill out all the forms alone will keep you busy for days, and the . . ." she seemed to give it up. "There are some men who come around regularly if you want anything. . . . But it's expensive. Do you know what they charge for a pound of coffee now? Three hundred lire. Well, let me know."

She took the empty tray and went out, shaking her head.

Three hundred lire for a pound of coffee! The equivalent of fifteen dollars. It was crazy!

"You see, I believe in the things I feel and see, but then, I am a little crazy," the man who had chosen to forget his name and wanted to be called crazy had told him. But it hadn't sounded crazy.

Was Pietro crazy?

Pietro, who had told him to go and see the Contessa San Vigilio – What else had he said?

This time Charles Barrett sweated all over. He reached into the pocket of his jacket, fumbling for a cigaret, but his hand came out empty. How stupid, he thought, wiping his forehead, how stupid of me to look for something that isn't there. But he would have given anything at that moment for a cigaret.

What if Pietro hadn't been crazy? What had their conversation been about?

Again he closed his eyes to shut out the room, the double bed which looked as if it would screech, the little writing desk in the corner with its plain stool in front of it, the rather ugly, faded wall-paper which showed fully grown roses in endless succession and the small piece of sky suspended blue above the window. He started trying to re-member every single word Pietro had said. Why, it had made sense! Exaggerated it had been, yes. Perhaps not the way an American would have ex-pressed his opinions, but definitely sane! But then, every crazy man had his bright and logical mo-ments when he perhaps saw more clearly and farther than many a sane person. He had behaved so strangely, though, been so hysterical, so easily excited. Dancing alone with his stick in the lobby. He could see him now, moving backwards, taking mincing little steps, his lips forming a silent whistle. And then all that silly talk the night Pietro had given him the idea of how to escape. Why, if he were to consider Pietro normal, then he would simply make a third in the ingenious net that had been woven about him. And Dr. Pederazzini would scarcely go so far as to involve a patient of his in this dirty game – make a sick person tell the things he was afraid to mention so that, in any case, he, Pederazzini, would be covered. . . . Possible . . .

Think carefully, now, Charles! You won't accept the first possibility, that of sheer mistake, so follow the second to its conclusion. If you have been planted in this position for the purpose of getting in contact with the Contessa, then, my dear old chap, you are under surveillance. Then every *carabiniere* and policeman, every secret German and Italian agent, knows exactly every move you make. Then you haven't the slightest chance of escape. In that case you will never be able to get a travel permit to Verona, or be able to walk on foot away from Rome to the Lake District of Northern Italy. You won't even be able to drink a glass of chianti in a restaurant without the whole gang knowing about it. You'd better get in touch with the Contessa at once!

As long as you do what they want you to do in

accordance with their plan, you will be relatively safe. It's up to you to play their game the best way you know how. To gain time. That's all that matters now. And to warn the Contessa. She . . . she's an American, too. She grew up in your country and she's in danger. If things are as you see them now, she's in great danger. . . .

Charles lifted the suitcases on top of the bed, which promptly screeched, and opened the smaller one of the two. He took out a clean shirt which was monogramed V.dP. and marked with the year 1939. Probably a way of checking up on the shop where it had been ordered as to whether it had really lived up to its promise of good material. Now, as he changed, he noticed for the first time how chilly his little room was. Instinctively he went over to the small pipes of the central heating and touched them. They were cold. And Rome could be dreadfully cold after sundown, even at the beginning of April. He had heard of all these things: no heating, or just for a few hours on certain days, no hot water to take a relaxing bath or a shower. He had accepted them as facts pertaining to a war-torn Europe, but he had never stopped to realize what they actually meant. Three thousand miles were not just a long distance, three thousand miles meant another world where people still had the necessities of life. . . . How smug

I've been, he thought, and stopped cleaning his shoes on the inside of the blackout curtain, which dangled like a little dark cloud from below the skylight right above the table. . . . Though I volunteered to fight for this very warmth and food and light, I just took it for granted that people were hungry and cold and dirty over here and never thought what the influence was going to be on the individual. . . .

He began to brush his jacket and his dark brown hat with the little brush which he had found carefully packed on top of his shirts. . . . And even if I am wrong, if I am just plain crazy in assuming that high politics are connected with my situation, anyway I should go and see the Contessa, he told himself. Because, after all, she is American born, and if she proves to be what I know her to be by reputation, she might be just the one to advise me. . . .

He walked out of the house and to the next post office where he took up the address book. . . . San Vercelli . . . San Villana . . . San Vigilio . . . Augusto San Vigilio, 13 Via Raimondi.

There they were. He looked again. There was no other San Vigilio. He went on staring at those letters till their print began to hop about. In his present state of mind he would not have been surprised to find that the San Vigilios did not exist.

Then he pulled himself together and walked over to the *questura* to ask for an application blank to fill out for his rationing card. It took him more than half an hour to get it. He had to stand in line, but he figured out that this would be what they expected him to do.

When he left the big building, he strolled along the Via Vittorio Veneto, past the Hotel Ambasciatore, where his American friends had stayed. Now an Italian and a German flag hung from the roof. Almost opposite lay the Excelsior which even six years ago had been the headquarters of German "tourists." Their large and pretentious cars used to stand at the curb, carefully guarded by doorman and chauffeur and the policeman at the corner, because all too often a tire would be mysteriously punctured.

The street looked strangely altered; it was almost entirely peopled with Germans of all ages and ranks. The little cafés on both sides, where he used to sit and sip his *apéritif* as he watched the people stroll by, had the sad look of trying very hard to keep up appearances. German was being spoken almost everywhere, sounding doubly harsh and clipped and alien in these surroundings. Once he stopped to look into the window of a shop where years ago he had bought delicious cakes and cookies and pounds of sugar-coated almonds. All he saw now were charmingly painted little boxes filled with tissue paper and fake candied fruit. But he also saw, mirrored in the window, the small *carabiniere* following him.

The man is just going home, he thought. . . . *The man is following you.*

He moved on quickly, pushing his way through a group of Italians, and disappeared into a house on whose second floor there had once been a famous *salon de haute couture*. The *salon* was still there, but the girl who opened the door to him as if he were insane said, "We have nothing. Not a thing. The Germans bought up everything. When the clothes rationing came, there was nothing left to ration," and she smiled as she slammed the door in his face.

When he reached the street again, the *carabiniere* was waiting on the other side of the street.

Charles crossed the place, and the Porta Pinciano which led into the Villa Borghese, Rome's Central Park, and moved quickly along a small path. Behind him he could hear steps. Twilight fell with wild suddenness. He stood still and lifted his head. Sometimes this same light would linger over New York, lending the city of stones a beauty and poetry which made one's heart ache. In a few minutes now, the sky, alive with green and pink and purple streaks as if a master's hand had brushed the paint across a huge blue canvas, would be completely dark. Then the lights would go on, spreading their glow over the remains of beauty and art and modern buildings alike. . . . But the lights didn't go on. Rome remained in darkness.

Charles walked more quickly now. Here and there in the night that had so suddenly fallen, he could hear voices. People were sitting on the benches. And behind him he could still hear even steps.

He took the short-cut through the Villa Borghese. He was sorry now that it had grown so late and too dark to walk up to the restaurant terrace to look over the seven hills and look down at the city.

Thirteen Via Raimondi.

Eighteen, seventeen, fifteen, thirteen . . .

He stood still. The street was deserted. He listened. He couldn't hear the steps any longer. Either the man who had followed him was standing still, as he was, or he had finally succeeded in shaking him off — or he was satisfied to have followed Vittorio da Ponte to the destination they had meant him to reach, and had withdrawn.

He looked up at the house but it was far too dark now to see even its outlines. Yet he knew what this house, Number thirteen, must look like.

One of those old *palazzi* built in the eighteenth century, with long, austere and beautifully proportioned lines which didn't betray what lay inside.

He groped his way through the night. A staircase . . . seven steps . . . and he was standing in front of the door. He stretched out his hand to find the bell, but the little button was apparently well hidden, as if ashamed of its modern origin, so he decided to use the knocker which he knew would be there, somewhere at the height of his chest. When he felt it, he was surprised to feel wood instead of iron or bronze. They had taken that away, too! His whole body stiffened. He had loved those little decorative antique things, which had been so much in harmony with style and taste — not important, perhaps, especially not to him; it was just once again the idea of what was happening to people and beautiful things. He knew, with a sudden deep, empty feeling inside him, that it had been his fate to come to this house. You're being silly, he told Charles J. Barrett of Tulsa, Oklahoma. Stop dramatizing yourself. Man is master of his fate. Since when have you become superstitious?

The knock sounded hollow against the bare wood of the door — the small bronze disc having also been removed — and rang through the dark, quiet street like the drumstick of some medieval town crier.

Charles stood still and waited. There was no answer. He leaned his head back against the heavy wood of the door, listening for approaching steps. Inside everything remained silent. He stepped back. But even if there were light somewhere, he would not be able to see it. The dark windows didn't tell whether, behind them, blackout curtains were drawn or not. Again he felt for the knocker and this time his fingers felt its outlines, a head of some kind, fastened to a wide ring, the head of a Medusa. He could feel the mouth wide open, petrified in its shriek, the long wild hair floating in single strands from her head. Probably a copy of the old one. He threw it back against the door, once, twice, three, four times.

This time he could hear feet moving toward the entrance. The door was flung open, a voice said, "Quick, Tina, turn off the lights. Come in, please."

Obviously the servant who had opened the door for him had expected to find someone else. He was an old man with silver-gray hair over the small, sad, intelligent face of a monkey. He wore a striped jacket over his trousers and a sort of gardener's apron tied over that. Not a regular servant, probably a gardener, or just a houseman . . . all that the San Vigilios had left of their former staff, untrained and decidedly startled to find himself face to face with a complete stranger who might have been a friend of the San Vigilios before he had had the honor of opening the door to his master's guests.

Charles quickly took advantage of this. He walked straight into the hall which rose through two stories. It was barely lighted except for a fire in the enormous hearth in which four men could have played poker without any difficulty. There was a large copper bowl on a three-legged stool in the room's center, in which, he could tell by the smell and the little smoke above it, charcoal was burning. It looked forlorn and rather like a joke in the tremendous hall. Charles quickly went over to it, took off his gloves and held his hands across the simmering pieces of charcoal. From where he stood he could see French windows which led into the garden at the back of the house, the staircase swinging into the hall at his left, the Gobelins which covered the walls.

"Is the Contessa at home?" he asked nonchalantly, still warming his hands.

The servant made no reply. Charles could hear him shuffle in his large worn-out felt slippers across the lovely black and white mosaic of the floor. . . . Ravenna, he thought; only in Ravenna have I seen such lovely mosaic.

"I am sorry," he said aloud, "I have no card with me. The paper shortage," he added, in a vague effort to excuse himself. But he knew that even that was wrong, that he would have dropped his card one Sunday morning when quite sure that the family was at church or out and that shortly after that he would have received a gracious little note from Luisa San Vigilio, telling him when she expected him, the exact hour and day, and the servant would have been instructed accordingly and would, at the mention of his name, have led him upstairs to his mistress.

"Will you ask the Contessa if Signor da Ponte may see her?"

The man stared at him, looking him up and down as if he had not heard right, as if he didn't understand. Charles saw his right hand move up to his ear, touching it, as if indicating that he was hard of hearing.

How old he is, thought Charles. Eighty. Maybe older. . . . And he repeated his request, this time in a louder voice.

Again the man looked at him as if he, Charles, had taken leave of his senses. Then he repeated slowly, "Signor da Ponte?"

"*Sì,*" said Charles. "*Da Verona.*"

The man nodded and moved away and was lost in the dark of the hall. Charles heard a door close.

He left the little bowl of fire and, pushing his hands into his pockets, walked along the whole length of the room to the fireplace. Now, close to it, he could see, in front of the hearth, a large, comfortable couch, not one of those graceful Louis XV sofas, but a couch, wide and deep, with slipcovers. Slipcovers, he thought — Luisa San Vigilio, American-born. Had she made modern furniture and slipcovers the vogue in Rome, defying its traditions of dignified, valuable furniture? Slipcovers, and Dad's last letter: "Your mother wants a new set of slipcovers for her birthday . . ." He smiled. He forgot where he was. He was back in the old frame house Dad had built for his wife when he had taken her away from the easy, gay, elegant life of New Orleans to Oklahoma, which had not been a state then. . . .

Behind the couch stood a large and very narrow refectory table, one perfect piece of wood on four heavy, artfully carved legs. On it, between some exquisite pieces of silver, lay a package of cigarets. His hand went out, quite unconsciously, quite mechanically; his fingers touched a cigaret, held it, pushed it between his lips, and, then, quickly took another and deposited that in the pocket of his coat. While he was looking for matches, he could hear voices arguing. A man's voice answering a woman. And then steps, light ones now. An elderly maid wearing a little cap of stiff linen on top of her gray hair approached him rapidly, followed by the slow-moving old man who was shrugging his shoulders and making vague little gestures with both hands at the same time.

"Signor da Ponte," said the woman, "I think you had better go . . . please."

"But," he said, "I have to see the Contessa. It is urgent! Please understand. Please announce me. I know this is not the time to call; but please, do disturb the Contessa and tell her . . ."

The woman pulled herself up to her full height. "Please *Signore,* come another time. Tomorrow."

"But I can't wait until tomorrow. Please," he said again, knowing all the time that he was baffling the two old servants by his way of explaining things to them which they must regard as none of their business, trying to break their obstinate clinging to rules and convention. "Please. I simply have to see the Contessa. Not tomorrow. Now. *Adesso.*"

"But you can't see the Contessa," said the woman, "because, you see, the Contessa is dead."

CHAPTER IV

THE Contessa is dead?" he repeated, drawing a long breath as if he needed all the air his lungs would hold, and grew silent, staring down at the black and white of the little square tiles of the floor. "When . . . when did she die?"

"Last week," the old maid answered, as she had answered so many questions, quite mechanically. But when she saw his face, she added, her eyes showing the weak glow of faint interest, "But you, *Signore* . . . you don't belong to the family?"

He shook his head. He didn't know what to say. This was something he hadn't counted on. It stunned him, as if he had received a blow.

"She was such a beautiful lady," the maid went on, her voice growing softer as memory overwhelmed her, "and so young still. Well, maybe God meant it well with her. Who are we to judge?"

This event threw everything he had figured out completely awry. Why, they must have known about the death of Luisa San Vigilio. Even if she had died suddenly, she had been dead when they had transported him to the Casa della Pace. So it was a mistake after all.

"I will come back tomorrow and see if the Conte has time to see me," he said hesitatingly, still wondering what he should do. Wouldn't it be best to discard everything else now and make definite plans for escape?

"Tina," called a voice. "Tina. Silvio. Where are you?"

The small door which led to the servants' quarters opened and in the full light of a narrow corridor stood a young girl.

"The Contessina!" cried Tina. "Using the back entrance just to save us some steps! Oh, why didn't you let us know that you were coming home for dinner? Nobody is home. The Conte phoned and said he still has to work, and Signor Arturo left half an hour ago, and nothing is prepared, no water heated for a bath, no dinner . . ." She talked rapidly, stumbling from one desperate revelation to the other as if her emotions were a whole long staircase she was tumbling down.

"Never mind," said the same restrained young voice. "Don't get excited . . . maybe we should keep that door locked – now. Just give me an egg and a little *brodo*. We have some soup, haven't we? And a little cheese and bread, and put it all on a tray and bring it up . . ." She yawned, coming closer, making a little noise like a sigh. Then she saw Charles. "Oh," she said, sizing him up with one look and deciding to accept him. "What do you want, *Signore?* I am Sybilla San Vigilio."

"I . . . I came to see . . . You see, I didn't know . . . I wouldn't have called otherwise . . . I am sorry I didn't know about the tragedy." He bowed and told her his name.

"Oh," she said again, and, as he had done before, walked over to the bowl in which the charcoal simmered. "Where did you find this, Silvio? I thought we had none." She spread out her hands while Tina and Silvio, apparently dismissed for the moment, hurried out of the room.

"Did you know her well?" she said. "She was a very lovely woman." For a second her voice seemed to break, but she caught herself. She looked at him, her face almost hard in the effort to keep its features controlled. "I am sorry. I didn't catch your name."

"Da Ponte. Vittorio da Ponte."

In the faint light he could hardly see her face. Only by her voice and movements could he tell that she was very young.

"Da Ponte?" she said. "Da Ponte?" She couldn't place him.

"*Da Verona,*" he said. "No. I didn't know her

very well. You see, I . . . I have lived in America for a long time and then the war . . ."

"America?" she said. "Really? I am partly . . . We are at war with America."

She walked away and over to the fireplace. "Do sit down," she said, turning the knob of a small lamp which stood on the table.

"May I, really?" he said. He was suddenly very nervous, suddenly very much aware of the fact that he had to act as Vittorio da Ponte in front of a young Italian girl. Why hadn't he gone immediately after Tina had told him that the Contessa was dead? Why had he stood there like a fool? How should he behave now? How could he possibly know how an Italian man would behave with an Italian girl? All he knew was that the men of this country were forever chasing foreign women while protecting their own from the slightest impudence, the merest approach. . . .

She misunderstood his hesitation and smiled fleetingly. "Without a chaperone? Well, you see, I have been brought up a little differently. Mother was American. And then . . . now there's the war . . . "

Again she looked at him. This time her eyes were on his civilian clothes.

"It's my heart," he said. "They couldn't use me."

She reached across the back of the couch for

the cigarets, looked at them — and then lighted one before he could pass her a match. He was blushing, and he knew it. Had she counted the cigarets? Did she know how many had been there? Would old Silvio be under suspicion now?

He said, "While I waited I must have smoked one, quite unconsciously," and he sat down opposite her in a deep easy-chair.

"Two," she said, and laughed. "War makes one stingy, doesn't it? Well, if you are so short of cigarets, I can lend you a couple."

Only now did he see that she was wearing some sort of uniform. He saw her inhale the smoke deeply and felt utterly embarrassed. She moved her hands up towards her head, the cigaret dangling from her lip, and unfastened a little white cap.

"Excuse me," she said, bent forward, took one or two pins out and began to shake her head till her whole face was buried under the suddenly loosened long black curls. Then she threw her head back, smoothed the hair across her temples and said, "Oh, that feels good. I am so tired."

She curled herself up in the corner of the couch.

"Maybe I'd better go," he said. "I . . . "

"I am sorry," she answered, sitting up straight again. "I must seem awfully rude, *Signore.* No. Please stay. I really want you to stay. It's just . . .

you see, I work in a hospital as a nurse's aide and there is such a lot to do."

He stared at her. Now, with the full light of the little lamp on her face, he saw that she was very beautiful. But – oh, of course, he thought, she would be. Second act of the play: boy meets girl. "You are beautiful," he said.

"I know," she said. It sounded neither bored nor arrogant. It just sounded matter-of-fact. Still, he must have looked slightly taken aback, because he saw her smile. "I mean, it's really nothing I'm responsible for, is it? And therefore I'm not proud of it. And I can't deny it – my mother was very very beautiful, and my father is one of the most handsome men I have ever seen, and they loved each other, so . . ."

Tina came in and whispered something in her ear.

"Maybe I'd better go now," he said again. "You want to eat. I heard you say . . ."

"No, do stay," she said again. "I'm much too tired to eat now. Tina, do we have some tea left? Make us a cup. And maybe you could talk to the bread and bewitch it a little so that it becomes a kind of toast." She smiled at him. "So now you don't have to feel obliged to make another move till you have eaten your toast."

"You are very kind," he said, a little stiffly,

guarding his words, trying not to translate from English.

"I am not kind," she said. "At this moment I am very selfish. You probably have an appointment and I am keeping you. But, you see, it does me good to look at someone for a change – who is whole. I mean, all in one piece."

He didn't know what to say, didn't know what she was expecting to hear.

"It's my heart," he murmured again.

"Don't excuse yourself," she said, lighting another cigaret. "A man would feel that way, naturally. Women don't. I think you are lucky. Now tell me . . . tell me about yourself." She was making an obvious effort to rid herself of the memories she had brought with her from the hospital.

"Well," he said, "I was born in Verona. Then my father died, in the last war, then . . . you see, he had a brother, so I left for America . . ."

"I used to go. Almost every year. What did you do there?"

"Studied. At Princeton. Languages."

He was mixing the lives of Vittorio da Ponte and Charles J. Barrett and he knew it, but he could not tell her that he had been confined for twenty-four years to an asylum. No.

"Yes," she said. "And then you came back. They always come back, the Italians. Maybe they don't like their nation so much as other people do, but they love their birthplace, don't they? Don't you? They hardly ever say 'I am an Italian.' They say: 'I am Roman' – 'Venetian' – 'I come from Siena' – 'Naples' – 'Florence' – but that is at any rate a patriotism that can do no harm."

They are district patriots. Pietro had said it. Now Sybilla San Vigilio was saying it. "When did you see my mother last?" she asked. "It's strange that we never met, not here, nor in America, nor on a boat. One usually meets the same crowd of people all over the world. When did you see her last?"

Six years ago, he thought. Careful, Charles!

He said slowly, "I think almost twenty years ago . . . yes. Almost twenty years. You were not even born then."

"I was three years old so I wouldn't remember you. But you must be making a mistake. You could only have been a boy then."

Vittorio da Ponte, born 1900. "I was twenty-three."

"You look younger," she said.

"Well, maybe I don't feel old."

"I feel old," she said. "You see, I was born here. I am twenty-three years old . . . and not married. The boy I was engaged to died two years ago. He was shot down."

They were silent. The wood crackled. Tina

came in with tea and some slices of bread, war bread, in which one could expect to find a blade of grass or splinters of some sort, considering what it was made of.

"I don't know," she said, "why I am telling you this." She looked up at him and suddenly she smiled, a sad little smile. "That's the war, too," she said. "It makes one feel more sensitive towards people. One knows right away whom one can trust and whom not."

He started to say something but she changed the subject before he had time to phrase his words.

"And what made you finally come here, I mean, after so many years, that you didn't forget Mother?"

He stirred his spoon around and around in his cup, although there was neither milk nor sugar. Once it clicked against the thin porcelain. "A friend of the Contessa, I think, more than anything else. He mentioned her name. He asked me to give her his best regards."

She looked up, interested. "Who was it?"

"He said, 'Just tell her Pietro sent you.' "

"Pietro," she said. "Pietro?"

He couldn't read her face. Did she know anything or didn't she?

"I don't know," she said. "Mother had so many friends. Not all of them remember us now." Her voice grew even lower. "We are not very popular

– oh, you know why. Did you ever really expect the United States to be at war with us?"

"No," he said.

"I didn't. Nobody did, actually. We believed in the threat – yes. But that it should become reality . . ." She put her hands around the little cup as if she needed all the warmth the hot dish could give her. Her eyes were very blue under her small curved shiny forehead. "Pietro . . . She used to call so many people by their first names or 'darling,' a habit she never lost. What does Pietro look like?"

"About fifty, I should say, or maybe a little older. Rather small, broad shoulders, a strong man, gray hair, black eyes . . ."

She stared at him. "No," she said. "I can't place him." She leaned back. "Probably just someone who admired Mother."

"He admired her very much."

She smiled. The smile was like a flash of light across her lovely, thin face. "And you did, too, didn't you? To be young and meet such a fascinating woman – it must have made a great impression on you. And what are you doing here? You look sort of lost. When did you come? . . . I am sorry," she interrupted herself. "I shouldn't press you, should I? And ask a lot of indiscreet questions. That, again, is the war," she said bitterly.

"We have lost our charm; we have become so blunt, so common, we even lose our manners. It seems just silly to have to bother with them when so many people are dying and — " She stopped abruptly. Something happened to her face which gave it the impression of a closed door.

"I . . . I am here on business," he said. "I arrived only today. As a matter of fact, when they asked where I was going to stay, I wasn't sure that I would get my reservation, so I mentioned your address."

"Oh," she said. "I see. And where are you staying?"

"At a little pension, Villa Elvira."

She shook her head slowly. Apparently she had never heard of the Pension Elvira. From far away came the sound of military music. She got up, turned out the light, and in the sudden darkness of the big chilly hall he could hear her move over to the window, could hear her low heels making a small clicking noise on the floor, the soft swish which the curtains made as they fell back into heavy folds, and how she flung the window open. The bars of a striking march could be heard clearly, the faint echo of horses' hooves touching the asphalt of the street and the dark, foreboding noise of marching feet.

He was glad now that it was dark because he

wasn't sure that he wouldn't have shown his surprise. Wasn't Rome supposed to have been cleared of military objects? Was the Duce taking advantage of this city's open status? There had been much talk of this very thing, yet, even though he had believed in the possibility, that was very different from actually hearing troops marching through the quiet of the Holy City.

She must have come back to the couch because her voice was very close. "More," she said, "more and more . . ." And it seemed to him that she was crying.

He didn't move. He didn't answer. Then, after a while, he went over and closed the window.

"Thank you," said Sybilla. "It did get rather chilly." She blew her nose and sighed. "I am very emotional right now. You see, I loved my mother very much. It was such a terrible shock. She was run over, you know. I had just left her. She had come to have lunch with me. She was so extraordinarily gay . . . for the first time since . . . since the war had started, really. You see, during the last years she was quite miserable. She didn't know what to do; she wanted to go back to her country, yet she loved my father so much she didn't want to leave him, and he couldn't go with her."

Suddenly she seemed to remember that she was talking to a perfect stranger, and though this stranger had known her mother and had not been afraid now to call on them, still, she was angry with herself for letting herself go.

She switched on the light.

He had been right, she had been crying. The shadows around her eyes had darkened and they looked softer and of a deeper blue. "Thank you so much," he said, holding her hand between his fingers a little longer than was strictly necessary, a slim hand with long fingers, their nails cut short and without polish. He could feel some calluses inside her palm. . . . She must be working hard, he thought. And suddenly he felt sorry for her. Standing there in the large, wide, cold hall next to the fireplace where the wood had burned away, she looked small and lost and sad. His glance lingered on her face, then he smiled at her.

"I hope I will see you again soon," he said.

On the left sleeve of her gray coat, which she had not taken off during the whole evening, was the wide black ribbon of mourning. "Yes," she said, rather flatly, as if she had suddenly lost all her energy. "Good night."

Silvio came in, as if he had been waiting behind the closed door for just this moment to let the visitor out. "*Buona notte,*" he said.

The door closed after him softly. Charles stood on the silent street, undecided where to go. He wasn't sure whether or not by now the park would be locked. Would the street cars be running in this complete blackout? He walked slowly down the Via Raimondi; he had forgotten the *carabiniere* who had followed him. At the corner of the Via Salaria he saw someone get out of a cab and ran up to take it. He decided, after all, to go back to the Pension Elvira. If they wanted to arrest him, they would find him anywhere just as easily as at the pension.

The small dining room was deserted and had not yet been cleared. It looked dirty and uninviting, with the chairs pushed back, tables standing at angles, the linen of the tablecloths soiled with spots of red chianti and soup, napkins thrown across them, glasses half-filled with water and wine. Anna, the maid, came in to turn out the light.

"I wonder if there is still something left for me," he said politely.

She looked cross. "Why, *Signore,* the kitchen closes at eight!"

He looked at his watch. It was eight-thirty. "If you could just warm up some soup . . ." He had a tip ready in his hand. "I'll carry it up myself."

"All right," she said.

She spoke the dialect of Piedmont, which was hard to understand with its special flavor — French words mixed in with Italian, and the quick sing-song intonation of the French. His mother had spoken French, had kept it up, always in the hope of one day going back to New Orleans and her childhood friends. He felt something akin to tenderness for fat, sloppy Anna.

He followed her into a small pantry, beside the kitchen. As he waited for the *minestrone* to be heated, he heard a terrific commotion, Anna yelling at the top of her voice, cursing, the sound of slaps, a boy's voice defending himself, then howling.

"Can I help?" he said, entering the kitchen.

Anna was standing there, holding a big brown hen under her arm. "Those devils! They tried to steal her again!" She was stroking its wings tenderly. "*Sì, sì, carissima mia,*" she told the bird. "She is the best one I ever had, Ambrosina is. Believe me, *Signore,* I couldn't live without her. I dread the day when I'll finally have to eat her, *mia Ambrosina.* Such a good little chicken she is, laying so nicely. I can almost count on three eggs a week. And good eggs at that!"

Charles went over to the stove, took a plate from the shelf above and ladled some soup into a dish. Anna was in no state of mind now to wait on him. "Where do you keep her?" he asked.

"In a nice big brown box right next to my bed,"

she told him. "But I don't know how to keep her safe now since they have taken the iron bars from the windows. The boys have tried to break in three times in the last month." She set the hen down on top of the kitchen table, seated herself in one of the chairs and stared at Ambrosina, her face wearing an expression of worship. "*Cara mia piccola, piccolina.* I have three nice worms for you."

Charles finished his soup. There were some vegetables left and some oranges. He knew how to bribe Anna. With the tips she could go and buy worms for Ambrosina.

He went into the little vestibule and found a chair next to one of the palm trees. Except for four people – three women and a man playing bridge – he was alone. Somehow, he dreaded going up into his room. His thoughts wandered back to Sybilla San Vigilio. He was almost sure that she didn't know any of the things her mother might have known. How strange that the Contessa should have died only a week ago. Why strange? he asked himself in surprise. Why do I think it strange for people to die?

Sybilla had been unexpectedly kind and frank. Why? Just because he had known her mother? Because he had called at a time when people with American relations were not popular if not suspect? Or because he had lived for so long in a country which she had loved because her mother had been born there? Maybe that was all. But maybe it wasn't. If she knew something – if she knew Pietro – would she have admitted that the first time she saw him? Wouldn't she be guarded before she admitted . . . admitted what?

Hey! He called Charles Barrett to attention. Watch out! What you are doing now is attaching too much importance to the words of a crazy little man who happened to have one bright moment. Can't you realize that this is all nonsense? You'd better think of how to make a getaway from here, how to dissolve yourself into thin air and leave Italy.

He found the cigaret he had stolen in his pocket and blushed again as he lighted it. One of the bridge players turned around as the thin cloud of smoke and the faint smell of tobacco began to float through the room, and eyed him enviously. He must have a lot of money, she thought, to buy from the black market, and she played a wrong card. Who was he anyhow? She had never seen him before. There were so few men left. Maybe it would be worth while to make his acquaintance even if he lived at the same shabby little pension she did.

Charles reached out to a stack of magazines

which lay on a table next to him and started looking at them to avoid any more attention from the bridge players.

So, he had been wrong all the time. His being sent to the asylum had been a mistake and the doctor had helped him to escape. He went back over all the things that had happened and the more he thought about them, the more he found himself coming to the conclusion which seemed the only logical one: that there was absolutely nothing to the idea of having been planted at Casa della Pace on purpose, that it had actually been a mistake. The Contessa was dead, Sybilla did not know Pietro.

He leaned back in his chair, realizing fully now what he had fought so hard to believe – that he actually had a chance of escape. As Vittorio da Ponte, carrying all the necessary papers of identification, there was nothing that could possibly hinder him from reaching the Swiss frontier if he did nothing to make himself conspicuous. It was quite natural for a man who had been confined for twenty-four years to want to go back to the house of his father, his house now. It was also natural that he would first have stopped in Rome to obtain all the necessary permits for this trip and to see the capital again with all the changes Mussolini had made in it. He would have to stay in

Verona for a little while. There was hardly any danger that anyone would recognize him. Vittorio da Ponte had left it when he was seventeen, going to the war from which he had come back a victim of shell shock. People who had known him would long since have forgotten him. Too much had happened in the meantime. And even if they did remember him as he had been, how could they tell what Vittorio da Ponte would look like after so much time had elapsed? But did he look like a man of forty-three? Nine years older than he actually was? Sybilla had told him that he didn't look his age. He wished he had asked her what she would have guessed him to be. But perhaps he just looked younger in comparison to the haggard, shabby, hungry, worried-looking people all around him.

Then he would want to make a little trip. Very understandable for a man who had been confined for such a long time to want to see something of the world he had missed. And since he couldn't do it by train without having to answer too many questions, he would make it on foot. Little Vittorio had always been fond of long hikes. . . . He smiled to himself. He would first go to the Lago di Garda. No time, though, to visit the charming little villages around the blue waters – Limone, where the lemons hung over stone walls, or Malcesine, on the other side, the picturesque little town where artists from all over the world came for the summer. Even Garbo was supposed to have been there. Brescia? Yes, that was on his way. He was glad of that. That drab little town housed in one of its churches one of the greatest masterpieces of the world, his favorite painting, a Titian. He closed his eyes and tried to remember the angel, the many different shades of white, the long robe, the beautiful wings, white, silver-gray, bluish white – the colors of peace. Somehow he would get to Stresa, the small holiday resort on the left bank of the Lago Maggiore where the conferences had taken place in 1925. He would visit the three famous islands opposite: Isola Bella, where peacocks promenaded amongst yellow roses; Isola dei Pescatori, with its many small restaurants and its little fishing fleet at the tiny port; Isola Madre, where a rich foreigner could rent a whole island consisting of a big old palazzo in its large park – for that was the Isola Madre. . . . Three little jewels; and, farther away, near the little town of Palanza, the small island with its white house hidden behind tall dark trees where Toscanini used to spend his vacations. On along the borders of the lake to Piaggio Valmara, the border: nothing but a small house on the highway, mountains to his left, the water at his right, the street hardly wide enough for three cars, and a sort of barrier, like the safety gates used to close a railroad track and, fifteen yards ahead, the Swiss border, an even smaller house and no barrier. At least, not then. . . . And before coming to the border, he would have to decide which way to take, whether to go across the mountains, along the old paths the smugglers used to use, or whether to swim across Maggiore, which narrowed here. How many yards could that be? A mile and a half? During the last war the lake had been carefully guarded, so he had been told; patrol boats day and night. No good. Better cross the mountains, he told himself. And then, if he made it, Switzerland, coming in at Ascona, a famous place now, frequented mostly by artists, in its atmosphere something like the Cape. Would Switzerland intern him? He didn't know. He didn't think so. Not when I come in civilian clothes, he thought. . . .

The woman looked at him again. She was about forty and not very attractive. Now she called out to him, "Do you play? You could cut in."

"No, thank you," he said stiffly. "I am sorry. I don't play."

He reached for more magazines. They were pretty old, some dating back almost two years. It was quite interesting to see what the Italians had considered right to publish then. . . . I need a map, he went on thinking. He was happy. He thought: Decent little fellow, that doctor . . . Suddenly he gave a start.

There, right in front of him, was the photograph of the man who had chosen to forget his name. A man in uniform . . . Pietro!

Charles put the magazine down on his lap. Then he took it up again, held it close, hid his face behind it. He read the caption: *Il Generale Pietro Vantoni* – General Pietro Vantoni. He looked again. Undeniably, it was Pietro. There was his face, the heavy Roman jaw, the curved nose, small dark eyes, broad shoulders, low build. Charles stared at the face, the face that had somehow been familiar from the first moment when this man had asked for permission to sit down on the bench beside him. And then Charles had discarded the idea of having seen this face before. Why? Because he had been influenced by his surroundings. Because it had never occurred to him that he might meet a famous general in a lunatic asylum. Pietro Vantoni had been a very famous man. He had become unpopular some time during the Abyssinian campaign, had been withdrawn, and then, later, when Italy had declared war, had been reinstalled.

Again Charles put down the magazine and turned the cover. What year had it been issued?

He looked at the table. The four were playing absorbedly now. The woman who had spoken to him said, "Well, I never double a little slam. It isn't worth while."

1942. July.

What had Pietro said? Or Bruno? Or the doctor? That the crazy little *capitano* had been at the Casa della Pace only eight months. Why, then, nine months ago Pietro had been sane, sane enough to be in command, sane enough to be given half a page in a leading magazine under the headline of "Leaders of Today" . . . Then Pietro had not lied when he had insisted that he was a general, had not lied when he had been working on his biography that evening and had told Vittorio da Ponte, "I was a general."

Charles slipped the magazine carefully under his arm. He got up, slowly, very self-conscious now.

"*Buona sera,*" he said politely, bowing to the four players. His voice sounded thick and unnatural to him. "*Buona notte.*"

"You're going to bed early," cried the woman.

"Early to bed, early to rise, makes a man healthy, wealthy and wise," he said.

She seemed to think this very original. "Well," she said, "you might look a lot healthier."

It's all right to look sick, he told himself. People

will jump to the conclusion that that's why I'm not in the army.

He walked up the whole three flights because he was much too excited to take the elevator. His body demanded action. In his room, he drew the curtain over the skylight and put the magazine on the table.

It was Pietro. Undeniably. He was not suffering from hallucinations.

What had Pietro said? Exactly? If he could only remember! Exactly!

He looked for some paper in his desk, but there was none. Of course not. He searched his suitcase. None. He went into the bathroom and came back with some. It would have to do. He found a pencil and sat down and began to put down the whole conversation as far as he could remember. What Pietro had said during the talk in the garden or in front of the little chapel or in the dining room was not so important – only what he had said after Charles had entered the general's room that evening counted. He read it, when he had finished, over and over again. . . .

Perhaps he had not put it down word for word, but this had been the crux of his words: there were important people, willing to help the Americans when they were ready to invade Italy. . . . There was a man who knew who these people were, who had a list. . . . "Go and see Luisa San Vigilio . . . just tell her Pietro sent you . . . she will help you . . . " What if all this which he had discarded as crazy talk were true? What if there were a number of people ready to help win the war for the Allies?

Come on, come on, Charles – what makes you think Pietro isn't crazy? Even though he was a general – what's to hinder a general going crazy? I should think it's only logical! All right. Pietro is crazy. He went insane shortly after this picture of him was published. All right. But he, like every other crazy man, has his bright moments. In one of those bright moments he tells you what he remembers. . . . He remembers that there are people willing to help. Never mind to what extent his mind has cracked – sometimes this poor mind remembers things; it remembered Luisa San Vigilio. Why should I jump to the conclusion that he is wrong in remembering a number of people who would be willing . . .

But if that is so – then . . . then . . .

He couldn't remain seated any longer. His whole body rebelled against inaction. . . . Then . . . Then I can't try to escape. Then it is my duty to find out whether Pietro Vantoni was having hallucinations or whether his memory was working right when he told me . . . Then I must stay here, in Rome, and find these people!

"Luisa San Vigilio . . . she will help . . ." But Luisa San Vigilio is dead! She died only a week ago. She died suddenly.

He stopped short. What had Sybilla said? "So suddenly . . . it was such a shock . . . she had been so exceptionally gay that day . . . you see, she was run over . . ."

Had the Contessa San Vigilio, American born, known for her Allied sympathies, died a natural death?

Hold your horses, Charles Barrett! . . . He threw himself down on the squeaking bed.

What am I doing? What am I thinking? Have I gone crazy really? Third act of my play – my little lieutenant becomes Sherlock Holmes, a master spy of political intrigue. God Almighty! I'm the little lieutenant, caught in a net, caught in this hellish European political net, mixed up with people who don't seem to know their own minds. They try wars to clarify things instead of talking them over. Caught between the Italians and the Germans; caught, caught, caught! I can't put this all aside and just shrug my shoulders and say, the hell with it, and make my escape, can I? I can't. I'm an American, I'm an American soldier; it's my duty to stay, to find out whether this is nonsense or – *very important.*

I don't give a damn for the Italians. I don't care what happens to them, nor to any people who are indifferent enough to let things come to such a pass; but if there are people willing to help . . . I can save American lives. I have to do it. There just is no other way out. . . .

But will America invade Italy? How do I know? I don't know the President or Mr. Churchill or General Eisenhower or anyone else. Maybe they will, maybe they won't. It doesn't matter. Sounds logical, though. Invade Italy . . . if they are going to invade the Continent, they may have to do it on all sides, through the Balkans as well as through Italy . . . And the British through France and the Netherlands. . . . What do I know about it all? I'm no strategist. I'm a little lieutenant who's learned by the sweat of his brow to march and salute and shoot and to obey. Maybe they aren't planning it. But maybe they would if I got back to them or could get a message to them telling them exactly . . . Maybe, on the basis of what I could find out, they would think it over. Then it would be important . . . *very important!*

He got up and looked at the photograph again. "All right," he said aloud to the picture. "I'll stay. I'll do my best."

There was nothing he could do until the evening of the next day when Sybilla would be home from the hospital. She was the only one he knew who might prove helpful. Again he wondered if she had any suspicion at all about her mother's sudden death. And if she had, would she tell him? No. Not unless she trusted him. And hadn't she said that war made you quicker to recognize the people one could trust?

He stayed in his room all morning, pacing the small distance between the four walls till word came from below asking him to please sit down for a while. After lunch he walked along the Corso Umberto, one of Rome's busiest streets, past the Palazzo Sciarra Colonna, a monumental building of the seventeenth century; then crossed over toward the church of St. Ignatz. Several monks stood in front of its Baroque façade. Glancing at them, Charles grew aware of the fact that he had missed the many monks of the various orders who, in their different-colored robes, more than anything else had brought home to the foreigner the realization that he was in the Holy City. He went to the Biblioteca Nationale, which was housed in an old gray building that had once served as a Jesuit college. There he finally found what he wanted — newspapers of the past few years.

He sat there for hours, reading carefully every news item he could find about Pietro Vantoni. But there weren't many. It seemed that the general had gone crazy quite unexpectedly and had had to be confined in an asylum. Not a single other reference. Every now and then Charles came across news items telling of United States failures, of terrible strikes, editorials that attacked the President in a scurrilous manner and extolled German efficiency and Axis victories, and he smiled grimly. They certainly could lie, these people, these governments that kept themselves in power by terror; and they certainly could make the newspapers lie, printing such falsified news, stupefying the masses. Well, one day the truth would be told.

When he came out and walked across the street, radios were blaring from all kinds of windows, shops, restaurants. Somebody was making a speech again. He decided to call Sybilla from the booth in a post office. It seemed safer to him not to use her telephone number where it could be so easily checked as at the pension. The more he thought about the Contessa's unexpected death, the more convinced he grew that it had been violently planned.

He could hear her catch her breath when he gave his name. "I would like to see you very much," he told her. "You were so nice to me yesterday. I'm feeling blue, and I'm lonely."

"I'm sorry," she said. "You see, I don't go out anywhere . . . now . . . "

"Oh. But I thought I might come and talk to you for an hour. Please. It's important."

"Important?" she repeated, a little startled.

"Important for me to see you again," he corrected himself quickly. "You . . . you matter a lot."

He heard her laugh—quick, unintentional laughter. "I'm not good company these days," and now her low, tired voice sounded a little gayer. "You really shouldn't bother with me, you know."

Charles didn't answer at once. Quite unconsciously he sighed deeply. "You aren't ill, are you?" she asked.

"No. I'd just hoped to see you . . . if only for a little while."

Over the wire he was always doubly alert to other people's moods. He could tell that she was hesitating. "I am lonely, too," she said solemnly, as if she were making a very important confession.

"And you don't believe in the old proverb that shared joys are doubled and shared troubles halved?"

"All right," she said quickly. "Come in for a bite of dinner. Eight o'clock. And don't be late." She hung up on him before he had a chance to answer.

Dinner, he thought. That was not what he had wanted. The Conte might be there, or some other member of the family he didn't know. For a while he reflected whether he should call her back and tell her that some important business appointment made it impossible for him to come at that time, or that something had come up . . . any lie. But then he decided that she would see through that, and that he'd better go. Anyhow, he would have to meet her father sooner or later.

Again it was Silvio who opened the door to him, but it was the Conte Augusto San Vigilio who greeted him.

"Signor da Ponte? My daughter told me that you called yesterday. I am glad to make your acquaintance."

He was a very tall and very thin man, immaculately dressed, elegant in his appearance, moving with the light grace of the Italian. What Sybilla had said yesterday about her father being "one of the handsomest men" had not been exaggerated by the love and admiration of a young daughter. He was strikingly good-looking. His eyes were blue and deep above a slightly curved, proud nose, his mouth almost too exquisitely cut, with wide sensuous lips, and his graying, bluish-black hair gave his head a quiet dignity.

Charles pressed his hand, murmuring that he had heard about the tragedy only yesterday. When they moved over to the fireplace at the far corner of the hall, he saw Sybilla sitting on the couch, talking to another man, similar in appearance to her father, yet much older. She addressed him as Uncle Arturo.

She wasn't wearing her uniform, but had changed into a black dress, a simple silk frock whose still lovely material clung to her body and showed the beautiful lines of her slim figure. There were some sweet Italian Vermouth and a little crystal *flacon* with bitters and some sliced lemon on a tray. She mixed him a drink and handed it to him, and for a fleeting second her eyes rested in his, smiling, growing bluer and deeper with their smiles. And before he could settle down, Silvio came in to announce that dinner was served.

The dining room was a very long and narrow room. The Renaissance table could have been set for twenty-four persons but now, with only four places, looked twice as long as it was. Several silver candlesticks stood on it, but only the ones between the plates were burning. They threw their flickering light across the high walls, bare except for one picture, a still life, and the massive cupboard. The chairs were small, with straight little backs and uncomfortable narrow seats. The Conte sat at the head of the table and asked da Ponte to sit at his right. Charles was glad to have Sybilla opposite him, to be able to look into her lovely face. Silvio put the plates in front of her and she began to serve the soup.

"Da Ponte, eh?" said Uncle Arturo, twisting his head around the big lights and addressing Charles. "Da Ponte . . . That name sounds familiar, somehow."

"Verona," said the Conte. "Didn't you tell Sybilla that you come from Verona?"

Charles nodded, trying to clear his throat, to say something, anything, quickly. He said, "What delicious soup. Really a great treat."

"Father went out to the farm yesterday. He is taking care of our estates now and he brought home the vegetables. Thank goodness, spring is coming, and we'll soon have more fruit and vegetables again."

"And meat at Vercellini's," said Uncle Arturo. "You know the *ristorante* on the Piazza Colonna? All the Germans go there, too, because of the meat, or the meat is there because of them. You don't need to say anything. You just order the most expensive dinner and under your salad leaves you find a surprise!" He chuckled to himself.

Silvio came in, carrying a large silver platter with the chicken, obviously also a trophy from the farm. Somehow the Conte did not look at all like a man who could lug food around. War did the queerest things to people . . .

"White or red?" asked San Vigilio, and began pouring the chianti.

"I've got it!" exclaimed Uncle Arturo. "Da Ponte. Francesco da Ponte. He came from Venice originally. He married Caterina Monte d'Oro. Don't you remember, Augusto? The Monte d'Oros from Turin. She was a lovely creature. Her mother was Regina. Oh, wait, now I have it! I knew your father. We fought together in the battle of the Col di Lana."

"Thank you," said Charles, reaching for the glass of wine the Conte was handing him. And, "Oh, I am so sorry!" He had spilled some of it, and a little white doilie of costly lace on dark yellow silk was stained with big red drops. They looked like blood.

Sybilla smiled. Uncle Arturo leaned back in his chair and let the chicken grow cold on his plate, apparently lost in his memories.

"That is a magnificent Urbino," said Charles, pointing to the lovely pottery bowl which stood filled to the brim with wild flowers between two candlesticks. For a second the strong clear colors of this sixteenth-century *objet d'art* actually succeeded in distracting him.

"He died, didn't he?" said Uncle Arturo. "I saw Caterina da Ponte shortly after his death. He had asked me to do so. You see, I had known your mother before she became his wife. They had one son. I think he volunteered and then . . . then . . . "

He stopped abruptly, then applied himself vigorously to his chicken. But Charles knew that the sharp little eyes were fixed on him.

"One son," the old man repeated.

"My brother," said Charles. "He died."

Sybilla let the lids fall over her eyes, as if she couldn't bear the word or any thought connected with death. Charles could see a slight tremor shake the Conte's right hand.

"And I always thought they had only one son . . . "

CHAPTER V

"HOW long are you going to stay in Rome?" asked the Conte, turning to Charles.

Why was Sybilla looking at him in such a peculiar way? "I am not sure yet," he answered.

If he could only think of something to talk about, something that had nothing to do with topics of the day, nothing about the war, nothing about the Germans, nothing about America. The conversation dragged along. Even Sybilla didn't bother to pick it up. He remembered how tired she had been the evening before and that for her to change her dress and sit through a formal dinner must have been a great effort. And then her mother had died so recently. All these facts were reason enough to prevent her from being a brilliant hostess.

Silvio came back and served *zabaione,* a sweet dish, eggs beaten with sugar till they were stiff enough for a spoon to stand up in them, and a few drops of Marsala wine for flavor . . . Uncle Arturo kept staring at him, although he was eating quickly and obviously enjoying his food which, thanks to the visit the Conte had paid the farm yesterday, was much better than it had been lately. Still, his glance remained glued on Charles.

He remembers correctly, thought Charles. The old fool! Why didn't he die years ago? He'll tell them. He'll tell the Conte and Sybilla that the da Pontes had an only son who had to be confined to an asylum because he lost his reason in 1918. She'll never want to see me again. I'll never have a chance to win her confidence, unless . . . unless I were to tell her the truth. But how can I do that? That's impossible! I wish he'd drop dead before the dinner's over!

Sybilla rose. "Let's have coffee in the library."

She led the way up the wide staircase and into a small library which had doors on both sides, standing open, one leading into a stiff little salon, the other into a study. There was a small cup of coffee for each of them and they sipped it silently, almost ceremoniously. The Conte showed him some of the books he had been collecting over a period of many years, beautiful first and rare editions, bound in white pigskin, printed on strong parchment, with artfully painted capital letters. Then he excused himself, saying that he had some work to do and would join them later. He closed the doors of the study behind him. They were alone: Sybilla, Uncle Arturo, and Charles Barrett.

"Do you play chess?" asked Sybilla.

Charles shook his head. Again he could feel the old man's eyes watching him.

Now Uncle Arturo said in French, speaking very deliberately, "Shouldn't you send Tina to bed?"

Sybilla looked at Charles. "We often speak French so that the servants won't listen to us." She took it for granted that he had been brought up with a knowledge of the language.

"You don't speak French, do you?" Uncle Arturo moved closer to him.

Charles thought quickly. Uncle Arturo might say something of importance in French which he wouldn't say if he thought Charles could understand. Charles shook his head. "No," he said. "I'm afraid I've forgotten all of it. You see, I lived in the United States for so many years that I had to learn English and that seemed to drive out the French." But he knew that Uncle Arturo, in his sly way, was laying a trap for him.

For a second the old man looked baffled. "Well, don't speak English here," said Sybilla quickly.

They sat around for a while longer, making small talk – speaking about the weather, the difficulty of getting food, the estates of the San Vigilios, and how because of the war they couldn't go down to Calabria as they used to do every summer for a few months. Then, when Charles saw Uncle Arturo look at his watch for the third time, he realized that he was supposed to leave. I guess I can't outsit the old man, he thought. And he's sure to tell her the minute I've gone. The only chance I have is to ask her some questions about her mother's death before I go. And then he remembered that yesterday, when Sybilla had used the back door to save the old servants' legs, Tina had cried out that nobody was home, that Signor Arturo was out too. Of course, her uncle lived with them.

He rose to say good night.

"I will see you downstairs," the old man said with charming, old-world politeness, moving surprisingly quickly.

Charles looked at Sybilla. God help me! he thought. Make her understand that I have to talk to her.

A faint smile fluttered across her mouth. "You stay here, Uncle," she said. "I'll see Signor da Ponte to the door."

"Look," he told her, going down the stairs, "you couldn't possibly take a walk with me, just ten minutes, around the block?" And, as he felt her body stiffening and saw her startled face, he added: "I really didn't see you alone for a second, did I, and I — "

"I'm sorry," she said quickly, her voice sounding almost tender. "It couldn't be helped. You see, Uncle Arturo didn't understand that maybe we two wanted to talk alone for a while." She blushed. "I mean," she corrected herself, "that even though one talks about the same things, one speaks differently, just two people."

"I am very glad I had the opportunity of meeting your father," Charles said, "but Uncle Arturo is a — "

"Uncle Arturo?" she said, hurrying to the defense of a member of the family. "He's a darling, isn't he? A walking *Who's Who*. What a memory the old man has!"

Yes, thought Charles bitterly, what a memory!

"Good night," she said, shaking him by the hand.

He made a last effort. "You wouldn't change your mind, would you? And talk to me for a moment where nobody could bother us? It's really quite important."

"Not at this time of night!" Again she sounded almost horrified. He understood. Never mind her American mother — she was too much of an Italian girl, brought up in Rome, to break conventions to such an extent. "I couldn't. Honestly. Don't look so disappointed, please. There'll be other times when we can see each other."

"Good night," he said, still holding her hand.

Between his large, strong fingers it felt like a frightened little bird, warm and trembling. For a moment he had trouble to restrain himself from the impulse to kiss her.

"Good night," she said.

Outside, on the dark street, desperation took hold of him. What if the old man told her . . . and how much would he tell? She would naturally never mention it, never mind how much she knew. But to him it was important to know exactly what was taking shape in her mind. He remembered the back door through which she had come, which she had said was open and should, perhaps, be locked. He went around the house, feeling his way along the walls, till finally his hands touched wood. The door had not yet been locked.

He did not hesitate. Noiselessly he opened it and went in. There was a long dark corridor with doors on both sides. One was standing ajar, and he could see Silvio sitting in the large kitchen, asleep on a chair near the stove. He passed another on tiptoe and could hear the sound of running water and guessed correctly that Tina was going to bed. Then he found the door which led into the hall. He could hear voices and stopped abruptly, pressing his body against the wall, making himself as small as possible.

Sybilla was calling "Good night" to her father.

From the sound of his voice, Charles guessed that the Conte had left his studio and was standing at the top of the staircase. Then he heard a door close. And then, Uncle Arturo's voice, calling softly to Sybilla.

"I thought you had gone to bed," she answered.

"I would like to talk to you, *carina.* That is, if you are not too tired."

"What about?" she asked. "Come downstairs. I'm just tidying. You can keep me company."

They were speaking French. Uncle Arturo said, "You will forgive an old man, won't you, for being tactless and indiscreet?"

There. Now it was coming. He wished he could see her face as she answered, "I don't know what you mean."

"You like that chap, don't you? Billa, *cara mia,* I mean the young chap that was here tonight."

"I don't know what makes you think that." No. She would not give herself away.

"Be very honest with me," Uncle Arturo went on, and his voice sounded grave. "I am not trying to probe, believe me. I would be the happiest man in the world if you could show interest in some-one else. Ever since the boy died, you . . . you haven't been well. You've been lifeless. And now, after the death of your mother, you haven't even cried. You are so hurt inside that you don't react any longer to anything, it seems to me. So nobody was happier than I when you told me last night about a man . . ."

"I didn't say I liked him particularly. I just said he seems to be extremely nice and well bred and understanding."

"But, oh, the way you said it!"

"Please, Uncle!"

"I know. I know," the old man quickly interrupted her. "Love grows slowly. It is not the time to speak about it yet, is it? Maybe in half a year, maybe later. But, you see, if you are interested in him, then I have to tell you something. If you don't care, even in the slightest, I will keep quiet."

Charles could feel his heart beat, knocking high up in his throat, making the blood pound in his ears. Here was his chance to gain her confidence. If she would just say, "I don't care a bit," Uncle Arturo would go to bed and not mention a thing. But if she said she didn't . . . then . . .

He heard her laugh, lightly, as though at herself. "Well, let's say I'm interested enough to hear what you think you must tell me if I'm interested."

"*Cara,* I hope you will forgive me for telling you. But you do remember, don't you, how nervous he got when I began to talk about his parents—his father, with whom I fought side by side; his mother; about the only child they had? He spilled some wine then, remember? And then, when he said he had a brother and that this brother had died — "

"I don't understand."

"You wouldn't. You see, the da Pontes had only one child. A son. He lied."

"But why should he do that? Are you sure?"

"Unfortunately, very sure. Because it was I whose advice was asked as to what to do with the son. His mother asked me. She wrote to me . . ." He stopped, drew breath and went on. "She wrote to me that her only son, Vittorio, had been badly wounded and — prepare yourself for a shock, my dear — had gone out of his mind."

Sybilla said nothing, nothing, at least, that Charles could hear. If she had gasped, the distance would have been too big to carry the small sound.

"They called in many doctors. They tried to hush it up. His mother was desperate. Then, when the doctors insisted on committing him to an asylum, she wanted to know which one I would recommend. At that time there was a very good neurologist, young . . . modern . . . I recommended him. Shortly before she died, I heard that he was still in the asylum near Anzio."

There was deep silence. Then Sybilla's voice, cold now with indifference. "Would you pass me a match?" And, after a little while, "So you think that this man is that Vittorio da Ponte. When did you say he was first confined?"

"Almost twenty-five years ago, I should say."

"Twenty-five years?"

"Undoubtedly he is cured, now," Uncle Arturo went on. "Otherwise they wouldn't have let him out. But, *carina,* you have to consider it. . . . Well . . ."

Silence again. What was she thinking now? Was she trying to remember the way he had behaved last night and today? He had to admit to himself he hadn't made sense.

"But he seemed so normal," she said. "So . . . so straight."

"*Poveretta.* Poor little darling."

"Oh, stop feeling sorry for me!"

"Do you remember how he said he had forgotten his French? Impossible. A man of his standing doesn't. He just doesn't. He told you he'd been away for many years, in America. That was a lie, too. He's been in the asylum all the time. If you don't believe me, I'm sure I can find out."

"Oh, don't bother. I believe you. It . . . it isn't so important. It's just that he was something whole. And now . . ."

"You aren't angry with me, are you?"

"Of course not. I am very tired. Do you mind if we don't talk any longer?"

Charles could hear the old man move; then it grew quiet except for Sybilla's steps making restless little noises across the floor. She was walking through the hall, back and forth, back and forth, like someone disturbed. And every one of her steps seemed to pound directly on his heart.

All he could feel, standing there, leaning against the cold damp wall, was the impulse to open the door which separated them, to run to her, take her in his arms and hold her close. To tell her that he was not Vittorio da Ponte but Charles J. Barrett from Tulsa, Oklahoma. But he couldn't. He was a soldier in the American Army, and though for the time being there was no one to command him and he was on his own, he had to act according to the principles of his country; even though he was not on the field of battle, he had to go right on making the same sacrifice millions of his comrades were making every day, had to be unselfish and put aside what was personally dear to him so that what was dear to all might live. Now more than ever, when fate had chosen him for a mission whose consequences in the present or for the future he couldn't foresee, could only sense to be of the utmost importance.

Her steps were coming closer, moving now straight in the direction of the door. He caught his breath. What if she came out into the corridor on her way to Silvio or to lock the little back door, and found him here? What would she think of Vittorio da Ponte caught eavesdropping? And for the first time he realized what he was doing and how it would look to someone who didn't know his reasons for wanting to listen.

The light from the hall hit his face directly as she opened the door. No use to turn and run. He stood and faced her. He could see her pale as she found him so unexpectedly opposite her. He spoke quickly and softly. "I forgot my gloves. I came back. I thought everyone had gone to bed. I meant to wake the servant, that's why I came to the back door, and it was open. So I thought, why wake the old man? I might just as well slip in and get them . . ."

"You – you are very considerate," she said, trying to compose herself. And then, with slight reproach, "But in the future, will you please ring? Never mind if the door is open or closed."

She walked away from him, as if she couldn't bear to be near him, as if somewhere, deep inside her, she were afraid of him. He saw her pull an old-fashioned, heavily embroidered strap which now, as in former days, served to set a little bell tingling. She doesn't want to be alone with me . . . He knew . . . She is ringing for Silvio.

It took quite some time till they heard a chair

being pushed aside in the kitchen and Silvio's slow steps coming closer. "Did you ring, Contessina? I am sorry. I must have fallen asleep."

"The *Signore* thinks he has lost his gloves here," she told him.

The old man went over to the little dressing room which was to the left of the entrance, where several hours ago he had hung Charles's hat and coat. "I am sorry," he said, when, after a little while, he came back to them, "I can't find any gloves. Is the *Signore* sure he left them here?"

"Quite sure," said Charles.

He reached into his pocket, instinctively and automatically, and when his hand came out, a glove slipped through his fingers and fell to the floor. He should have made himself familiar with the contents of Vittorio da Ponte's pockets.

"I am so sorry," he said. "Will you forgive me for all this disturbance?"

"It's quite all right," Sybilla said, her voice tired now. "Will you show the *Signore* out and lock the door, Silvio? Good night." And without looking at him again, she began to walk up the staircase.

He called her early the next morning. Silvio told him that she was at the hospital and could not be reached. He went and bought some flowers, a little straw basket painted white, filled with violets that were the color of her eyes. He wrote a little note, excusing himself again for his behavior, assuring her that only consideration for the old servant had made him enter her house again without being admitted, asking her to meet him soon and, for God's sake, to let him know when he could see her again. At six o'clock, after a long and lonely day, he called again. This time Tina answered. She was sorry, but the *Signorina* had just come home and was lying down. She had left orders not to be disturbed.

He finally reached her next morning, just before she was leaving the house. She answered the telephone herself, probably expecting it to be an emergency call, not prepared for the fact that a man would dare to call at that hour of the day – six o'clock in the morning.

Her voice was even and kind, as if she had made up her mind to treat him like a patient, a sick man, best handled softly and patiently, but firmly. It infuriated Charles, but he kept his temper. "I do have to see you," he said.

"I am afraid, *Signore,*" she answered him quietly, "you have met me at a very unfortunate time. I am very depressed and in no mood for a flirtation. You will surely understand that so shortly after my mother's death . . . I just . . ."

But just because she had felt so lonely, just because her mother had so recently died, she had given him a chance the very first day they had met. She had changed her mind, or, better, Uncle Arturo had changed it for her. What girl would allow herself to fall in love with a man who for twenty-four years had been out of his head, even if she had felt attracted to him at first?

"Please let me see you."

"I am working very hard," she said, "I have very little time to myself. I will let you know when it is more convenient and we will have dinner together." Again she hung up on him before he could say another word.

He had called her from the public booth as he had done before. He went back to the Pension Elvira. He was utterly depressed. She hadn't even mentioned his flowers, nor his note of apology. . . . Skip it, he told himself. You are no longer fourteen years old. . . . But he couldn't skip it. It wasn't as simple as that. Not because he was a young man who had fallen in love, you could call it that to give it its simple name, but because Sybilla San Vigilio represented the only possible link in the chain which had been broken by her mother's sudden death . . . She was vital for what he had come to consider his supreme mission. He needed her letter of recommendation to people her mother had known. He needed her to find out those persons who had been friends of Luisa, the friends who had not ceased to come and see her regardless of her unpopularity since the war with the United States. She, Sybilla, had to tell him, she or her father would have to bring them together – he had to see her again.

After lunch, he walked to the house in the Via Raimondi, carrying a big bunch of red roses. He was lucky. Silvio, and not Tina, opened the door. Would Silvio give these flowers to the Contessina, *prego,* and could Silvio possibly tell him at what hospital she was working and when she usually left it? He pushed a hundred-lira bill discreetly into Silvio's veined hand with a smile. Silvio smiled back.

"*L'amore, l'amore,*" he ventured to say, and giggled. "*La primavera,* Signor da Ponte."

"Yes. It's spring," said Charles.

Sybilla worked at the Ospedale Umberto, and usually left at five o'clock by Entrance 2. He buried his hands deep in his pockets and walked away quickly. Spring. Yes. Such a decisive spring. For so many people perhaps the last spring. For the first time since he had come to the city, he went sight-seeing as he had done the very first day he had been in Rome, a young man industriously studying his guidebook, so eager to take in everything of unbelievable beauty there was to see. And, as he had done then, he walked up the wide staircase which led to the Piazza del Campidoglio, flanked at its top by the statues of Castor and Pollux; greeted again the statue of Marcus Aurelius, sitting proudly on his horse. He, indeed, had been a great man, an intelligent soldier, firm and sharp, and at the same time one of the wisest and kindest emperors in history. He walked across the large, wide, round Piazza, another proof of Michelangelo's genius for line and architecture, and looked down at the miraculous sight of the ruins of the Foro Romano: the three last remaining, high Corinthian marble pillars of the temple of Castor and Pollux mirrored in the long narrow basin of the Vestals. For a moment he forgot that there was a war, forgot that he was a soldier on a dangerous mission, forgot that all over the world people were dying, and fell into a trancelike state, relaxing completely in the face of such beauty and grandeur.

Shortly before five he was standing opposite Entrance 2 of the Ospedale Umberto in the Viale del Policlinico. He watched the soldiers moving in and out of the big modern military complex of the barracks next to it. He could hear sharp commands coming at short intervals from the drill ground in its center. Then he saw her coming, pushing her way through the revolving door.

"Sybilla," he said. "I had to see you."

For a moment it seemed as though she wanted to go back in, then she shrugged her shoulders. A frown showed on her round, shiny forehead. She looked at him crossly. "I don't like to be waylaid," she said, and added, obviously remembering that she should treat him gently, "I am in a hurry to get home." She started to walk quickly.

"Let's try to find a cab."

She stood still. "I prefer the streetcar," she said.

He realized that what had induced her to come to a standstill was the streetcar stop. "I must have a talk with you," he said.

The streetcar came and she swung herself onto the little platform. People from behind pushed him up. The conductor let an incredible amount of people get on before he pulled the bell for the driver to go on. They never got to hanging onto the straps. It's like Times Square, rush hour, thought Charles. He could hardly breathe. Around him everything seemed to smell of garlic. One poor little mother was picking off from her baby's dirty woolen blanket some fleas which seemed to have dug in for the duration. Charles, his knees pushing against her bony legs, watched her pick out the fleas between thumb and forefinger, break them in two with her dirty nails, and then just let them drop to the floor. Eleven bodies farther away he could see Sybilla's little cap waving like a small white flag between other heads.

The streetcar stopped at the Corso Italia — more people seemed to get on; stopped at the Piazza Fiume — he raised himself on tiptoe to see if she had escaped him; and, finally, at the Via Salari. Here she was pushed against him. "This is where I get off," she said.

From here it was exactly two blocks to the Via Raimondi, hardly enough time to say what he had decided to tell her. "You wouldn't walk with me into the park, just for a few minutes?" he asked, breathing deeply.

She shook her head. "I am sorry, *Signore*. I have to go home. Another time."

He looked around. There was nobody to be seen. He put his hand on her shoulder, already turned away from him, and felt it stiffen under his hand.

"Don't be afraid," he said, whispering in English. "If I had been crazy, how could I have picked up English? In an asylum? You don't believe that, do you? If I were lying, how could I know that the Sixth Avenue El was torn down in '39? How could I know that your mother was born in an old-fashioned house on the Marina in San Francisco, that Mrs. Roosevelt has rented a house down on Washington Square . . ."

"Careful," she said in Italian. Two people were passing them.

"Will you walk with me in the Pincio?" he said in Italian.

"*Sì*," she answered. "No. I think you'd better come home with me. You always wanted to see my room, didn't you?"

They walked the short distance to the house silently. Silvio winked a vicious eye when he saw them coming in together. Her room was very big, sparsely furnished, a big fourposter bed, a writing desk, the walls lined with books, a fireplace, and two easy chairs.

"Please make yourself comfortable," she said, and went out. When she came back, she nodded. "It's all right. Nobody will listen."

He said, "Your uncle told you about Vittorio da Ponte? Are you afraid? You see, that's why I suggested the Pincio. I thought maybe . . ."

"I don't understand," she said, staring at him. "Not only do you speak excellent English, you speak it the American way. Yet you speak Italian as I do, as any Italian would."

He broke into a Southern drawl, "Why, sugarfoot," he said, "Ah'm suah glad you think so," and changed his voice again, into the soft singsong of New Orleans. "Madame, please do believe me."

"Who are you?" she said.

"Never mind," he told her. "I am an American. And if you make one move, Sybilla, you won't get far!"

She lighted a cigaret nervously.

"I don't understand," she said. "I don't understand."

"Don't try," he said. "You see, if your uncle hadn't talked, you would probably never have known anything about me. You would have continued to know me as Vittorio da Ponte, and that would have been perfectly all right with me. But he did talk. It took me two days to make up my mind to tell you the truth. Because otherwise you won't help me. And I need your help."

"American," she whispered. "We are at war with America."

Her lips grew white. He saw her fingers which held the cigaret shake. "If . . . if you were in my place, if I were to meet you under the same circumstances in America — what would you do?"

"That's simple," he said. "In my country you wouldn't even be an enemy alien as long as you were loyal to our democratic ideas, as long as you were on the same side of the fence."

She was silent.

"You see," he said softly, "I think that any person raised by an American, who has had the chance to compare, to travel and see democracy at work, would want to carry the torch of liberty for equality, for humanity, for the peaceful development of civilization. Maybe I am not a good judge of human nature, but I had the impression that you were on my side. If I am wrong, if you should decide to give me away, it might not just be I who would die, but hundreds of other people."

"I won't denounce you," she said, and her voice was flat, without any tune. "Because of my convictions, which – you are right – are the same as yours. But help? You spoke of helping just now. I couldn't help you to kill the people of the country of which I am a citizen." She shook her head violently.

"Of course not," he said. "I wouldn't ask you to do a thing like that. What I am asking you is not to betray something, but to help me to help this country of yours. Help it to end the war, help to save it from more bloodshed, help to free it from the Germans, help it from being completely destroyed."

She sat down. "How could I?" she said. "I am a girl who knows nothing of politics."

"Sybilla," said Charles, getting up and crossing over to where she sat, putting his hands on each of the arms of her chair. "Tell me, honestly, do you think your mother died a natural death?"

Her eyes grew big with terror. "What makes

you think that?" she whispered. "What ever makes you think that?"

"You have wondered about it yourself," he said.

She raised both hands to her face and buried it behind her fingers.

"Tell me exactly what you know about it."

She was trembling so violently now that he walked away and over to the window to give her time to compose herself. After a little while her voice came, hardly audible, "We had lunch together that day, I told you that already, I think. She was extraordinarily gay. After lunch she always liked to take a walk in this neighborhood, sometimes through the park. She loved to walk."

She stopped, caught her breath, then went on bravely. "A German car ran over her, a military car, speeding . . . The driver was arrested. He claimed that she could not have seen him coming, that she crossed the street the very moment when . . . She died before Father or I could get here. You see, it happened just at the entrance to the Pincio, only a few blocks from here, and the policemen knew her and brought her home. Tina called her doctor. He was the last one who saw her alive."

"What is his name?" asked Charles.

"Lorento. He has known her all her life. I mean,

ever since she came to this country. Father and I asked him if she said anything before . . . but he said she died so quickly . . ."

"And where is Lorento now?"

"He has been commissioned, in spite of his age. They need doctors so badly. He has gone."

"Where to?"

She shrugged her shoulders. "I wouldn't know."

"Sybilla," he said. "What made you think that it was not an accident?"

"I couldn't say," she replied slowly. "Naturally, Mother was not very well liked any longer after the war started. She was so well known for her democratic convictions and her love for America. You see, she could never quite make up her mind what to do. On the one hand she wanted to go back, but she didn't want to uproot Father. So they stayed. Father used to teach at the university because he believes in education and that the more chance people have to know about things that matter, the better the world will be. He resigned before they could force him to leave because of Mother . . ."

Charles sat silent for a moment. The last man who had seen Luisa, the doctor whom she had trusted, to whom she might possibly have given a message, was gone. Impossible to trace him.

"Do you happen to know who she saw that day

you had lunch together, or the day before that? I mean, because you say she was so exceptionally gay."

Sybilla thought for a while. "No," she said finally. "I don't know what she did on those days. I mean, she always only told me what she wanted me to know or what she thought might be of interest to me. And I was so busy at the hospital. No. I don't know."

"Sybilla," he said softly. "I have reason to believe that your mother was murdered, brutally and purposely murdered."

She stared at him, wide-eyed. "Why?"

"Because there are a number of important people who would be willing to help America end this war more quickly. Perhaps your mother was connected with them."

Her voice sounded far away. "There has always been a large group," she said, "intellectuals, teachers, ministers and many among the Navy, who are antifascist. But they have all been imprisoned or sent to the Islands, exiled . . ."

"Perhaps they are not the same ones any more. Still, there are these people and, as I said before, I have reason to believe that your mother knew them, or that they trusted your mother because she was an American and wouldn't betray them. You see, I think your mother, the Contessa Luisa

San Vigilio, was a . . . well, let me call it a key man in these circles."

"Why?"

He moved closer to her and settled himself in front of her on the floor. "Does the name Vantoni mean anything to you?"

"Certainly. He was one of Mother's best friends. That is, he was, before he went crazy. You see, he quarreled with them all, he had grown very unpopular; then I think he refused a commission. That was when they found out that he was insane."

"I see," he said. "Well, as your uncle told you, I was confined to an asylum. There a crazy little man mentioned your mother's name, made me promise to go and see her."

"Tell me," she said, "tell me everything."

He turned his head and looked at her till her eyes were caught in his glance. "You know you can trust me," she whispered, "don't you?"

Maybe it was the way she said it which all of a sudden created a world of intimacy. From one moment to the other, they ceased to be merely friends or just people sharing the same interest, and became, instead, a man and a woman who knew that love between them was only a question of time and conditions. Again he looked at her. What had happened between them and when had it happened? At a moment not even consciously grasped?

It was so much easier now to speak to her. He said almost lightly, "It will sound perfectly fantastic to you. Sometimes I wonder if it wasn't all a nightmare or something I have written up as a possible plot for a play. You see, I'm a writer. Well, this is what happened to me."

He told his story quickly. Once or twice she made a little noise or exclaimed in a low voice full of surprise, "Oh, no!"

"That's the truth, the whole truth," he told her when he had done, "and it led me to the following conclusions. First I thought that I was being planted here to be used for a certain purpose, perhaps to act as a decoy for your mother, but later, when I heard of her death, I came to the conclusion that someone, somewhere, meant to give me a message."

She got up, pushing her chair aside, and now she began to walk the floor. "Yes," she said. "That is the only logical explanation. Vantoni must have known something of what Mother or other people were thinking and planning and remembered in a clear moment, and told you."

She came back and sat down on the floor next to him. Their shoulders touched. "What is your name?" she said.

"Vittorio da Ponte," he answered, staring into the cold fireplace in front of them. "Let it go at that."

"If you wish it."

He nodded silently.

Outside it had grown dark. The evening wandered across the sky. A church bell chimed. A pigeon cooed somewhere. "What do you want me to do?" Sybilla said.

"I have to find the man who has been chosen to take your mother's place, or the most important of them all, directly – the one who could give me the exact names."

"Yes. Of course. But how?"

"I haven't thought of a way yet," he said. "Maybe I never will. Maybe someday somebody will contact me. I don't know. I don't even know if we are on the right track. Well, anyway, I want you to go over your mother's diaries, her notes, her engagement books. I want you to write down the name of every person she used to see, let's say during this last year, and perhaps we'll find a clue."

"I will," she said simply.

Suddenly he heard her crying, softly.

"Hush, baby," he said, as if she were his girl. "Hush, baby. War is a stinking thing, but we are in it, and we have to get it over with once and for all, and if we can both help do that, well . . ."

He put his right arm around her trembling body and made her head rest on his shoulder. He held her loosely, tenderly, with a tenderness he had never felt before, and which surprised him by the great warmth of feeling with which it filled his heart. Her little white cap slipped off the back of her head and fell to the floor, but neither of them bothered to pick it up.

"You are not alone any more," he told her, whispering into her ear. "You aren't alone any more with your fears and your longings and your dreams."

Under his lips he could feel her mouth curve into a smile.

After a little while, she rose. "You must go now," she said. "We have guests for dinner. And I can't ask you to join us. Uncle Arturo wouldn't understand." She smiled. "But usually they leave early, at about ten o'clock. If I have a chance to get away, I'll meet you, just for a little while. I can't promise. You understand? In the meantime I'll try to find Mother's notes. I'll look through her desk."

"Where would you want to meet me?"

Through the darkness, their eyes met. "You must be careful," she said. "Promise me to be careful? I think you are relatively safe, for the moment. . . . But still, you are in great danger. If they should find out, you wouldn't be made a prisoner of war again – you are a civilian now. They would shoot you as a spy."

"You mustn't worry," he said.

"If you are right, and my mother had connections with certain people, and was killed because of that, someone may be watching us, Father, and me, the whole house."

He thought of the little *carabiniere* who had apparently followed him on his first visit to the house in the Via Raimondi, and the other one, the first one, to whom he had given the address. ("San Vigilio, eh?")

"No. You mustn't come here any more. Meet me at the Fontana di Trevi, at ten o'clock."

In summer, the Fontana di Trevi was the poor man's Atlantic City: the large, famous fountain with its low rim, situated on the south side of the Palazzo Poli, and the wide steps that led up to the church of St. Vincent and Anastasius, on which, on hot nights, people of all ages sat: young mothers bringing their children along, holding the last and tiniest on their laps, old men falling asleep, young boys and girls talking of love, women gossiping, knitting rapidly – all of them waiting for a slight breeze which would make the waters spilling across the blocks of granite under Neptune's feet spray through the air. A thin veil of millions of little drops, bringing a moment's refreshment and the illusion of coolness . . . Years ago, on his way home from little *ristorantes,* Charles used to stop there and sit among the people, listening to their quick and witty chatter, watching lovers of all classes and ages stop in front of the basin and search their pockets for a piece of paper and a small coin; fold small boats with clumsy or already accustomed hands, put the lira into them, carefully—ah, so carefully—and set the little boat with its cargo out into the water, watching it eagerly, their breath held. Because, if the little paper vessel sailed safely across the small basin toward the two stone goddesses of Health and Fecundity without sinking or coming undone, the wish would be fulfilled. . . .

Charles waited for over an hour, but Sybilla didn't come.

CHAPTER VI

HE wasn't worried. After all, she had said, "If I have a chance to get away, I'll meet you . . . I can't promise. You understand?"

No, he wasn't worried. For the first time since he had awakened at the Casa della Pace, he felt almost happy. Now he knew definitely that he was on the right track. He felt sure that he would somehow find the person in question and would get the important list. Maybe it would take some time, but during those days he had something else to think about. Sybilla. Billa. "Billa," he told the soft air of the night. "Billa . . . Billa . . ." And then he felt embarrassed. Oh, hell! What I need is a drink to get myself straight! One didn't walk around like an eighteen-year-old kid, one's girl's name on one's lips as if it were something to be tasted. Or did one? He stopped at the corner of the Via Boncompagni, which ran into the Via Vittorio Veneto, right at the side entrance to the Excelsior. Why go anywhere else? From here it was just a few steps to the Pension Elvira.

At the bar, where he had so often sat drinking whisky, there was quite a crowd. When he came closer, he saw that nearly all of them were Germans. His teeth set hard. There they were, the Huns. His enemies. And he, Charles J. Barrett, right in their midst. What a situation! He almost smiled. He leaned against the door and his eyes wandered across the room and back to the bar, searching in vain for the man he had known as bartender. Old George was no longer there.

Charles withdrew into the big, rather elegant lobby, and seated himself in a corner. So it was true what Jackie Loft had told him, that George had had to go because he preferred to serve the Italians before the Germans. He glanced around the lobby which lacked any special characteristic and could have been in any first-rate Continental hotel. The waiter who came to take his order didn't look Italian to him. Did they bring along their own staff, he wondered? They would! They didn't trust anybody and nobody trusted them. He asked for some Vermouth and then sat quietly, watching German officers wandering in and out of the lobby, the way they carried themselves, so stiffly and self-consciously, their stomachs pushed out and their shoulders drawn back. Among them were some men in civilian clothes and others in the black uniform of the S.S. He watched their blunt, crude faces, their heavy jaws, the flat backs of their heads. One of them had given the command to run over the Contessa Luisa San Vigilio. What strange and cruel people! How was it possible that men like Beethoven, Goethe or Schopenhauer had belonged to this race? But, maybe, he thought, maybe that creative and constructive class of people had never really had any influence on the German masses, maybe they were so small a class that they really didn't count among the Prussians, who needed war to prove themselves superior, who had to destroy in order to justify themselves. He paid his small check and went out quickly.

Upstairs in his room, he found that he wasn't sleepy. He was excited. . . . Calm down. Calm down, he told himself. You'll have your chance to get your hands on them yet. He started to walk up and down, but from below somebody hammered against the ceiling and he threw himself on his bed. A terrible and cold hatred grew in him. He hated them, no longer out of sheer principle and clear, logical thought, but quite personally; hated them because they made him, Charles Barrett, not only want to kill them, but destroy them as a race!

He must have dozed off, because when he heard heavy banging against the door, heard voices and quick steps echoing from the small entrance up to the third floor, he did not connect these sounds with himself. He sat up, rubbing his eyes like a small boy disturbed in his first, deep sleep. But then, when he heard the elevator hum and a voice calling out "Guard the staircase!" he jumped to his feet. They were coming for him! And before he had time to jump onto the rickety table and try to escape through the skylight, the door was flung open. Two S.S. guards, accompanied by a young Italian policeman, stood on the threshold.

"Hands up!" one of the S.S. men ordered, speaking Italian, bad Italian, harsh and clipped. The other man moved, apparently to search the room. The little Italian stood guarding the door.

Charles thought: Sybilla. She didn't come to the Fontana di Trevi. She has denounced me.

The man who had spoken was tall and heavily built, with the face of a butcher. How many people had he shot, how many unnecessary brutalities had he committed, in order to prove that he was worthy of becoming a member of the S.S.? He held a revolver in his short, chubby hand and came closer now, searching Charles, his hands moving across his chest and hips expertly and quickly. "Move!" said the same voice; and Charles felt a kick against his shins and at that moment he saw red.

How many years had it been since Charles Barrett, just for the fun of it, had taken up boxing? He didn't know. All he could remember now were the precise and expert movements of the jiujitsu which had been a part of his basic training as a soldier. His right foot shot forward, unnoticed by the man, and caught him. Charles's arms came down like a flash; one reached for the heavy water-bottle on the table, the other twisted the man's right arm, making him drop the pistol. The bottle came down on his bald head and he fell to the floor, moaning.

The little Italian didn't move. He stood and stared, surprise written all over his young face, too startled to shoot. Why, he had come to regard his German colleagues as a sort of Supermen! When Charles's left swung against his weak little jaw, he fell immediately. After all, it wasn't his duty to pull himself together when the Supermen couldn't.

It had all happened in a flash. There was a pistol on the floor. Charles and the other S.S. man made a simultaneous grab for it. At the same time the S.S. man fired his own. The bullet whizzed by Charles's left ear, whistled, and stuck in the wall. Charles felt the muscle of the man under his hands, strained and big in the effort of wrestling, below the cloth of his uniform. He threw his whole weight against the man, got him under, and knocked the big red head in hot blind fury against the bare floor until it grew limp and the body gave in. The man had fainted.

Charles jumped across the body, kicking the Italian who blocked the threshold out of the way. There was the staircase, and another man coming up it. He waited till the man had reached the top and then flung himself on him. As they rolled down the stairs together locked in a furious embrace, he again could hear the elevator buzz. More were coming up, or down – he couldn't tell. He only knew that, three or four steps below him, there was a curve in the stairs, with two heavy posts in the bannisters. His right leg shot out, his foot caught hold, his calf twisted around the first post and he had the advantage. Bracing himself with one hand against the wall, he let the man topple over his left leg and kicked him in the belly, sending him rolling down the entire flight, moaning, only half conscious. Charles pulled himself up and vaulted across the bannister into the well of the staircase, landing on the ground floor just as the elevator started upstairs again. The front door stood open. From outside he could hear the noise of a motor running. He ran into the little lobby, which was dark and deserted, pushed open the door that led into the pantry and kitchen, and from there ran to the back door. It was locked, but the key hung next to it, just as he had seen it hanging the evening when Anna had prepared his soup.

His bruised and trembling fingers managed to get the key into the hole and to open the door. The small courtyard outside, where carpets and furniture were aired or beaten and some laundry was always hanging out to dry, was surrounded by a small wall. It was easy for him to pull himself up and swing his body on top of it. There, for a moment, he paused, listening, and through the small distance to the house, he could hear excited voices. One rang out. "He can't get away. The whole quarter is guarded."

He let himself fall behind the wall. His feet touched soft ground — a garden. In the pitch-darkness he couldn't see a thing. Yet he ran. His head hit a tree and then his hands felt another stone wall. This one was higher. He made it, and had to stop for breath. Now, through the night, the humming of two or three motor bicycles was clearly to be heard. He saw the quick, sharp light flash through the dark at his right. Another wall, and another; now cobblestones under his feet; a courtyard, a low fence, and, from high above him — voices coming from the roof of a neighboring house. He threw himself flat on the ground. His face fell into something soft, something wet. Leaves, damp with heavy dew – and for a second he could smell the sweet fragrance of violets not raised in a hothouse. Violets . . . He lay there panting, keeping his body stiff and still. He had sent her violets, a little white straw basket of violets, and she had betrayed him.

Several flashes of light and then, again, darkness.

The blood was pounding in his ears. Carefully he moved on. A gate, one of those little gates that lead into a small garden, locked only from one side by a wooden bar running across it diagonally . . . He opened it noiselessly. Beyond it lay the street, dark and apparently empty, yet still filled with the sound of running engines.

The strong smell of incense came to him and he realized where he was – right next to the church of Trinita dei Monti. He started to run again, taking the steps of the Spanish staircase two at a time. Escape was all he could think of, escape at any price!

Hide. But where?

His brain was working quite automatically now as if, set running by emergency, it could remember all the things Charles Barrett thought he had forgotten. The small narrow streets running into each other, through which he had had such trouble to steer his little car; the Balilla . . . where were they? Somewhere in the neighborhood of the Pantheon. Piazza Colonna, he thought. If I could reach the Piazza Colonna, I'd have a chance!

His body moved on as if it were a magnet being drawn in the right direction. A big, wide square . . . Don't run, now. Walk quietly. Walk very quietly, like a tired man going home. Keep close to the houses. Don't cross the Piazza, even if it costs you several minutes. A motorcycle and a car, their sirens shrilling . . . steps echoing, a guard of four . . . *milizia* or *carabinieri* . . . Where was there a niche? All the old houses had niches. There must be a niche! He caught his breath and stood quietly. They passed him.

He listened to the echo of their vanishing steps. I'd better take my shoes off, he thought. With them on, I can't run. With them on, my steps echo. . . . He bent and took them off, tied them together and moved on, almost on tiptoe.

A couple he couldn't see, in front of him, a girl and a boy, talking: "I don't know what happened. This is the fourth time they've stopped us. Something must be going on."

He withdrew into the wide entrance of a house, moved on, tried to think, tried to time himself. Any moment now, he should reach the Piazza Colonna. Between it and the Pantheon, he would have a chance. There were less cars swishing around now, no more flashlights, less patrols, or so it seemed.

A voice called, "Halt!"

Too late. He had not seen them, had not even heard them. He pushed his shoes inside his jacket. A flashlight fell on his face for a second. He could see two guards, their long, elegant coats floating behind their backs.

"*Carta d'identitá, prego.*"

The "please" behind the order gave him courage. His hand fumbled in his pocket. They mustn't notice his hand, they mustn't see it bruised. He felt the gloves in his pocket and managed to slip one over his right.

"Here," he said.

The flashlight lighted up his photograph, glued to the paper Pederazzini had handed him.

"This is the third time I have been stopped on my way home," he said, putting enough curiosity into his voice to make it sound natural and indignant at the same time.

"Well," said the man, "we are just doing our duty." He handed back Charles's papers. They walked on.

Charles bent down, took out his shoes, pushed his hands into them and made them move, regularly, evenly. Then, when he felt sure they couldn't hear him any longer, he sat down on the curbstone and put them on again.

He walked on. And again a smell came to him through the dark of the night to orientate his senses: the poor, dirty smell of a crowded quarter, garlic and onions and the water used for washing, carelessly poured away onto the cobblestoned street. Arms outstretched to both sides, he could feel the walls of the houses to right and left. . . . Hide, he thought again, hide anywhere till I can get my bearings, till I can make a plan. . . . From above there came a sad little noise, the night wind playing with the laundry which was spanned across the narrow street from window to window, smelling of cheap soap. Who had once called them the flags of the poor?

Hide. But where?

There was the tiny square, the Piazza Capranica. Was there a little restaurant on it? He couldn't remember. And he knew he wouldn't find it if it was there with everything blackened out. And what use would it be except for a moment's rest? To sit at a table for a minute, order some chianti, and think quietly . . .

He listened for voices which might penetrate the curtains and glass, but all he could hear was a man cursing from an open window on the second floor of a house, and the crying of a woman. Then he remembered what Anna had told him, that the boys had tried to steal her good hen, Ambrosina, by slipping in through the cellar windows from which the iron bars had been removed to be used for ammunition.

After a few moments of search, he found such a window. He kneeled down, feeling the sharp, uneven stones cutting his flesh. Here, where he was now, there was no curbstone. The doors of the houses led directly into the street, into traffic and all. He lay flat, trying to push in the glass without making any noise. But breaking and entry had not been a part of his education, he had not learned to push in windows soundlessly. The glass splintered, fell inside, making a tinkling noise.

He stood up quickly, listening into the dark, then walked nonchalantly away a few steps – in case someone might have heard and might come to see what was wrong – as if he had had nothing whatsoever to do with it. But everything remained quiet except for the noise from the open windows above him. . . . The man was hitting the woman now . . . a few dull, heavy blows echoed above him. But if anyone but he heard them, nobody was doing anything about it. The neighborhood knew this couple, their regular fights. They had long ceased even to gossip about them. They had their own fights.

Then, when he dared, he walked back. This time he threw himself flat on the ground, his head out into the street, his feet pushing into the window's maw, deeper, deeper, till he could feel the frame touching his ribs. His hands grasped it and for a second his body swung above unknown ground until he let himself go.

Hands and feet touched what he had anticipated at the same time – the hard cement floor of a cellar. He straightened out and breathed deeply, once, twice – ten times, till he could feel his heart quiet down to a calmer rhythm. He moved cautiously, walking alongside the wall. His outstretched right hand touched something ice-cold, wandered over the shape of it . . . a nose . . . closed eyes . . . a pouting mouth. His head moved and hit against something. Marble, he thought. A figure. Now he felt its contours, a fat little behind, a small body, large outstretched wings – an angel. One, two, three figures . . . probably the storeroom of a dealer in graveyard statues. Finally he found the door which led into the cellar. It was locked. He felt his way back. The figures stood so close to each other that there was hardly any room to sit down between them. He had to move several little cherubs before he could stretch out, his head resting on the arm of a small cross. He took off his jacket, rolled it up and pushed it behind his neck, there where the cold hard granite pressed against his bones. Now, lying almost outstretched, he relaxed for the first time. And, relaxing, he felt his whole body ache. Again he got up, forcing himself to do some exercises. I need my muscles, he thought. They mustn't grow stiff. He went on bending his body, moving his arms and legs till he could hear the blood pounding in his ears again. Then he lay back and closed his eyes.

If only he had a match, to see! Match, he thought. If only I had a cigaret! "So," he told himself in a whisper, "she denounced me after all!" And the moment he said it aloud, he knew that she hadn't done it. Then why had they come? Why had they sent three men to arrest him? And others to guard the house he lived in? If Sybilla had not betrayed him, then what had happened? He lifted his hands to his face and began to massage his forehead. Think. Think clearly, he urged himself on. It seemed to him that never in his life before had he had to do so much thinking and figuring out as during these past days.

For a while he was too exhausted to form a clear thought. His mind hung in a vacuum, empty, drained of all intelligence and intuition, only his heart and his instinct kept telling him that she couldn't have done it. He started repeating to himself the words they had said to each other, starting from the end of their conversation and working backwards, a game he had played with himself so often when he had wanted to check up on things that had been said and what thought or word had led up to another.

There was only one possible explanation – he set his teeth, making a slight, ugly noise as his jaw closed hard – that they had watched him waiting outside the Ospedale Umberto for Sybilla, seeing her home, entering the house with her, staying there for an hour or two . . . and had come to question Sybilla.

His mouth went dry. Behind his teeth his tongue lay like a piece of thick heavy meat. He couldn't move it. He parted his lips, trying to breathe. Then Sybilla was in grave danger. They who had so callously murdered her mother wouldn't hesitate to – to torture her if they thought she knew something.

His eyes began to burn in their sockets. They would have questioned her . . . again and again. She would have refused, once, twice, maybe for a whole hour, and then she couldn't have stood it any longer and . . . Nobody who hadn't been through it himself could possibly know how he would stand up under it. And she was only a woman . . . a girl . . . a kid!

"I am lonely, too." He thought he heard her voice, almost ashamed to admit it, yet with a tune of happiness in it that there was someone whom she could trust. The way her head had felt against his breast . . . So small . . . The smell of her black hair, tickling his chin . . .

Unconsciously his fingers formed fists. He hammered against the hard floor in a fit of desperation. . . . No, no! he thought. How could she have kept silent? How could she have kept on refusing, denying questions?

And at what point would they have been satisfied with her answers? What had she confessed when finally she could not bear it any longer?

He forced himself to stand up and walk to the window and back to the place where he had rested, to drive the vision of her suffering from his mind. How much could she have told? How much had he told her? Slowly, now. How much had he told her? He hadn't mentioned his name. Nor the Casa della Pace. Nor that of Dr. Pederazzini.

Vantoni. Pietro Vantoni was the only name he had mentioned. What could she have said? "A man, a Signor da Ponte, came to see my mother. He didn't know that she had died. That's all I know."

"Strange that he didn't know of the death of

such a well-known person. Where did he come from?"

"My uncle recognized him as the son of a dead friend who had been confined right after the last war."

"Where?"

"I don't know."

She wouldn't have told more. She might have said, "You see, he was embarrassed at having been confined for such a long time. He didn't want us to know. He pretended it was his brother . . ." She would not have said more. He knew it. But would her interrogators have been satisfied?

"God!" he said aloud. Hard as he was fighting, he could not keep his fancy from painting horrible pictures. Pretend, just pretend to yourself that this satisfied them. You'll go crazy otherwise. . . . Then, most certainly, they would have proceeded to arrest him, to question him, while, at the same time, they were probably checking up at the asylum where Vittorio da Ponte had been confined twenty-four years ago. But why, then, had they questioned her at all? Why not him directly? If they had watched him, they knew where he lived, where they could find him. Why then put a girl through such a beastly cross-examination? Into his mind slipped the face of the German captain waiting in front of the Casa della Pace, and the way it had looked later when the same man had addressed him . . . the faces of the German officers at the Excelsior Hotel . . . the faces of the S.S. men coming to arrest him . . . He shivered. Sheer brutality. To see a lovely young creature wince . . . To prove to themselves once again that they were almighty and could do whatever they pleased . . . No. There was more to it than pure sadism. There was system behind it. To let him know that she was in their hands, that by confessing he could save her, to make him unsure by telling him that she had said this and this . . .

He lay on the hard, gray floor, his face buried between his hands, his whole body shaking with the tears he couldn't cry. Then, after a long time, he grew quieter, harder, and into this calm the thought came to him: Perhaps they did come directly to me. . . .

Go to sleep now, he ordered himself. You are a soldier, and soldiers must learn to sleep before the battle. Forget everything that is not connected with your goal. Go to sleep for an hour, and then, while it is still dark, get out of here. . . .

Half-past four in the morning. Charles stood at the window, listening for the noise of steps, when all of a sudden the door behind him opened. He had been so tensely listening for any suspicious sounds from the street, that he had not heard the small noise of a key being pushed into the hole. Now, apparently lighted from an outside switch, two bulbs hanging from chains threw their light over the many figures as well as on him.

"What are you doing here?" a man's voice yelled, and he could see a fat little man step back into the corridor.

"Don't yell for help!" Charles said quickly. "I'm not a thief."

"Then what are you doing in my cellar? And you broke the window."

"Here's some money. I think enough to fix that." Charles held out a bill. The man lost his fear and moved cautiously closer.

"What are you doing in my cellar?" he asked again.

"I . . . I wanted to hide," Charles said, watching the man out of the corner of his eye. "I . . . you see, I had a quarrel with a German."

"With a German, eh?" said the man, and stepped closer, almost snatching the money from Charles's hand. "That's bad business," he said. But his eyes were smiling.

Charles turned his hands, swollen and bruised, his thumb hanging strangely from his right.

"Broken, eh?" said the man. "Well, I hope you didn't let him get away with nothing."

"On my word of honor," Charles fell easily into the slightly proud bragging the man seemed to expect, "if that devil dares to face the world today or tomorrow – maybe it will take a whole week till he dares show himself again – I'm no true Italian!"

The man touched his hand. "Needs fixing, eh?"

Charles nodded. "Tell me," he said. "You wouldn't know a place to hide for a day or two till the storm blows over?"

The man looked silently down at the bill he still held between his fingers.

"I would be willing to pay well for it," said Charles.

"You can't stay here. You see, I've got to ship some of these figures my brother-in-law makes out to the cemetery. He'll be here in a moment with one of his men to help him. You'd better come along before they see you."

Behind him Charles went across a passageway into a courtyard around which the house was built – balconies on each of its floors, the different floors connected by an outdoor staircase, like a fire escape, thought Charles – and into another entrance at the other side of the court, and from there into a small stable.

"Nobody will look for you here," the man said

"Got something to eat?"

Charles pulled out another hundred-lira bill.

The man closed the heavy wooden Dutch door behind him. Charles couldn't tell whether he had nodded or not.

It was a small stable, with one or two little wagons in it, like those the Italian peasant uses for driving into town, to bring his vegetables to the market. But where there should have been, over the primitive seat, the little roof which folded up or down according to its owner's wishes to keep sun or rain away, the material had been removed. There were two stalls. One housed a meager little mule, kicking nervously and bad-temperedly, the other one was empty, with some sparse remains of dirty straw on the ground. The walls were high and gray, with a small window set so high that he couldn't reach it.

Charles stretched himself out on the straw. He took his money out and pushed it into his stocking. No use falling asleep and waking up to find himself robbed.

Through the opening, one could hardly call it a window, he watched the day dawn. All sorts of noises came to him: children waking up, men and women running up and down, using the community water tap on each floor to fill their pails with water for the stove, or washing their faces and hands right there, on the spot, growling like angry dogs when a hurried housewife would push them aside. The heavy wooden wheels of a cart rolled into the yard. Now they were loading the figures on it . . . now they were quarreling about the price of the fare. Then everything grew quiet.

A big fat fly hummed around him. He was too tired to catch it. He saw a thin rat pop through a hole in the outer wall and run to shelter across the stable. For the first time in his entire life, he had lost his sense of humor completely. Not a joke was in him, nothing of his spirit was left which could ridicule him and his present situation. Charles pulled his lower lip through his teeth till it hurt. . . . A man who can't make fun of himself any more is lost, he thought. Where can I turn? I can't try to get in touch with Sybilla, nor with Pederazzini; all I can do is hide, here and there, wherever I can get to. All I can hope for is that they won't get me. It's even of no use to plan escape any longer. By now my description has probably been given out all over Italy. The only chance I have is to walk up to the next policeman and give myself up, to tell him that I am an escaped prisoner of war, that I made a getaway as soon as I was put into the receiving camp, that I used the name of da Ponte because I found it in a telephone book . . . something like that.

And that I went to the house in the Via Raimondi because I had known the Contessa several years ago when I first came to Italy on an exchange scholarship.

This was his only chance to escape death. He knew it. He sighed. He felt like a deserter, like a man running away from the battlefield. . . . One can't accomplish every task one sets out to fulfill. Be sensible!

Be sensible?

He sat up with a start. Were those millions of peoples — in the air — on the battlegrounds — in the Navy — in the Merchant Marine — sensible? What if they thought as he did now, and went home and said, "War isn't sensible. We don't want to go on."

He felt the blood surging up into his face from the roots of his heart. . . . Coward! he said to himself, slowly, disgustedly. Charles Barrett. No one is forcing you to desert. And you can't give up, that's all there is to it! You just have to keep going and trying to find out what you can! If they get you — all right. That's just your rotten luck. All you have to be sensible about, right now, is to see that they don't get you!

He heard a noise at the door and started, but it was only his royally paid host who entered. He carried a mug of lukewarm milk, two hard-boiled eggs and a handful of nuts. He sat on his haunches watching Charles drink and eat.

"My name is Mario," he told Charles. "You want me to bandage your hand?" It was surprising how soft and expertly his clumsy-looking fingers moved.

"*Grazie mille, Mario.*"

"Why aren't you in it?" asked Mario. He had nothing to do now and he liked to talk.

"My heart."

"With me it's my lungs," confided Mario. "It's in the family. Lucky, ain't we? I, and my boy, and my brother could stay at home, and my brother-in-law, too. He limps. My daughter is working in a factory and my wife is dead. Where did you sock the soldier?"

Charles pleased him by making up a beautiful fight and describing it in detail. After that he felt he had earned a reward. "Look," he told Mario. "I would like to sleep for a couple of hours. I didn't get much rest between your statues last night. They were pretty hard."

Mario laughed and coughed a little at the same time. "But do me the favor and wake me about noon, will you?"

"Sure, I will. And don't worry, *amico*. You are safe here, safe as in Abraham's lap."

When Mario came back and shook him by the

shoulder, the sun stood high. Charles could tell at once that something had happened. There was nothing kindly and talkative any longer about the man with the sick lungs. He seemed somehow angry. . . . Frightened . . . that was it.

"You'd better get out quick," he said shortly. "And don't you dare let on where you hid yourself till now. Understand? I don't know you! I never heard of you!" He was almost shouting now. "I've never seen you before! Understand? Now get out! Quick!"

Charles held his breath.

"Look," said the man. "I don't like the Germans either, never have. I'll be glad to get rid of them and never have to lay my eyes on a single German again as long as I live! But that's something else than what you've done . . . "

"What are you talking about?" said Charles.

The man snorted with anger. "Telling me that you'd socked a soldier! A fine story, that! And I, stupid fool that I am! I'm so proud of you, I laugh!"

Charles brushed little wisps of straw from his jacket and trousers. Only now did he notice that his jacket was torn and that there was a hole in his trouserleg.

"You wouldn't help me fix this, would you, Mario?" he asked.

The man shook his head stupidly. "I tell you, I don't want to be mixed up in anything like this. Not me! I have one boy and a girl; I have a family; I can't afford to . . . Get out!" he said, lowering his voice. "Get out quickly before I call the police and have them arrest you!"

"All right," said Charles.

Mario stepped aside to let him pass, not stirring from where he stood. But when Charles reached the door, he called out, "Be careful. It's in all the papers, you know."

It made Charles turn around abruptly. "Papers?" he repeated. Would they really put a story of this kind in the papers, make it public? No. He was sure they wouldn't. Unless . . . unless they had arrested them all. But even then . . . That wasn't the way they played this game. They would never mention it, hush it up, and would remain, in the face of the world, a united Italy.

"What is in the papers?" he asked.

"About the bomb and everything."

"Bomb?" he repeated, stunned. And then, quickly, "Mario. You've got a paper? Well, then run out and buy one quickly. Bring it here. I must see a paper. Quick! Quick! Run! Don't you understand me?"

Still Mario stood motionless, his face sullen, his mouth almost pouting with startled indignation.

"Quick!" Charles repeated. "If you don't go and get me a paper, I'll shout at the top of my lungs that you've hidden me here in the stable, that you bandaged my hand and brought me food."

"You pig!" said the man, but he went.

Bomb, thought Charles. Bomb? I've had nothing to do with a bomb. . . . He heard Mario coming back, throwing the paper at him as if having it handed to him would have been asking too much. There it was. Somebody had planted a bomb last night in the cellar of the Excelsior . . . luckily it had been found before it had exploded. . . . Now the police were searching for the man. Last night they had encircled the whole quarter adjoining the Excelsior Hotel and had searched all the small hotels and pensions for possibly suspicious persons. A raid!

Charles didn't read any further. He dropped the paper and it fell to the floor.

A raid, he thought. So it was a raid. They didn't know a thing about my real origin, they didn't connect me with the San Vigilios, they didn't question Sybilla about me. They just encircled a certain quarter in which, so it happened, my pension, the Pension Elvira, was situated. I, who had been sitting in the lobby of the Excelsior – it is probably well guarded, full of detectives – just happened to be one of the suspects. . . . They didn't come to arrest Charles Barrett. They came to arrest Vittorio da Ponte, a man whose name they probably didn't even know when they came for him, whom they just happened to watch leaving the lobby of the Excelsior and walking the small distance over to the Pension Elvira. If I had gone with them quietly, I could probably have cleared myself. I could have asked to be identified by the San Vigilios as a friend of theirs. They would have let me go after a day or two. What a fool I've been! What a God-damned fool!

He began to whistle with excitement. It's all my fault. My fault entirely. Instead of trusting Sybilla, instead of thinking twice before acting, and letting myself be taken away, I jump to the conclusion that she has betrayed me. The little lieutenant, reading mystery stories, novels about spies. It's always the woman, in them. How could I ever get the idea that she had broken her word? How could my brain have been so fuzzy that it couldn't think of anything but escape, escape at any price? Because I thought that all was lost . . .

"Eh?" said Mario, who had been pretending to tend to the mule. "What do you say now?"

Charles answered impatiently, his voice thick with fury at himself: "Oh, leave me alone. I've got nothing to do with it. Stop worrying!"

When did I lose my nerve? he thought. When exactly? When that German bully kicked me. That was the second when I stopped being smart, when everything in me revolted, when I couldn't help myself. And now I've ruined everything.

I've made myself suspicious, and I've committed the crime of resisting arrest.

He sighed so deeply that Mario turned around to look at him. Charles began to laugh, the bitter, hard laughter of the realization of one's errors.

His brain began to work fast. Casa della Pace, he thought. I must try and get back to the Casa della Pace. Vittorio da Ponte has been ill for so many years, it is not so extraordinary that he should suffer a relapse. The excitement was too much for him. It's all very understandable. He who hasn't had a drink for so many years took one or two that evening. Then, when they came to arrest him on a routine raid, his mind snapped. Dr. Pederazzini can fix it. I've got to go back to the Casa della Pace. Maybe they can still use me.

He walked out of the stable, past the startled Mario, without once looking back, without a "Thank you." He walked through the courtyard and through the main entrance onto the street and around the next corner and into the first little restaurant he could find, straight into its telephone booth.

Silvio answered. "The Contessina? She is at the hospital. She said to tell you, in case you should call, that she would give you a ring as soon as she got home."

So it was all right. There was no connection. The Casa della Pace was still safe.

He left the restaurant and walked along the streets till he found an old taxi. "To the golf links," he told the driver. He couldn't risk taking a train. He would have to walk the rest of the way. It shouldn't take him more than one or two days. Somewhere on the way there he would get himself different clothes, would do something about his hair and face, maybe. He leaned back in his seat. He had certainly been lucky to find a taxi to take him as far as the Via Appia.

Sybilla, he thought again. She is safe. Thank God, she is safe. I was having hallucinations last night. Overwrought, that's what I was. They wouldn't dare touch her. The Italians wouldn't let it happen. Her mother – yes. She was American. Yet even against her they didn't dare make a case. It took the Hun to find a way of getting rid of her. . . .

The taxi stopped abruptly. The driver turned around. "Sorry, *Signore,*" he said. "You'll have to get out. I've run out of gas." He began to swear softly under his breath. "They cheated me. *Si-*

curo! Or somebody pinched some of my gas. No lock is safe nowadays."

Charles handed him the fare. He looked through the open window. They had just made the Via Vittorio Veneto. The traffic was heavy. He stepped out of the cab and mixed quickly with the crowd. He hadn't walked five yards when a hand came down on his shoulder. A voice said, "You are under arrest. Follow us quietly."

On either side of him stood plain clothes men. There was nothing he could do but obey.

The cell into which he was thrown after they had taken away his papers, belt and shoelaces, was very small. Yet it housed three other people: A very old man who looked like a shriveled old lemon and sang all the time; his voice carried no tune at all, it was nothing more than a loud and penetrating whisper that his throat formed, and it sounded dreadful, as if all his vocal cords had been cut. A peasant, surprisingly tall and strong and gentle in his movements, like a child, perfectly aloof in his prayers. And a small boy, a Sicilian, not older than seventeen, who sobbed incessantly.

They paid hardly any attention to Charles when he was pushed into their midst, only looked at him for a second, moving automatically closer to each other to make room for him on the stone bench which ran along one of the walls. The cell was horribly bare: four naked walls, dirty straw, blankets on the floor, the bench on which they sat, and a table with a pitcher for water which was empty. The window was so high over their heads that even by climbing onto the table they could not have seen outside.

Charles didn't know where they had brought him. They had put him into a car which had stopped two street corners farther on where he had been transferred into a prison car. Then, after quite a while, handcuffed to one of the plain clothes men, he had been led down long corridors where their steps had created a hollow echo, till finally he had been taken over by two guards, led along more corridors, down several flights of steps, until he had reached his destination . . . this cell.

After a little while the boy turned to him and said in a low and desperate voice, "I've been here for nearly five months. When will they get around to me? The prisons are so crowded. They have arrested so many people. The guards tell me they don't know when my trial will come up."

"What are you in here for?" asked Charles, watching a rim of sunlight wander across the stone floor.

The boy shrugged his shoulders. "I don't know," he said, in his slow, desperate voice. "I think I must have said something . . . something about that I don't see why we should fight and that maybe I wouldn't go if they drafted me."

The peasant interrupted his prayer. "I killed a man," he said. "I never meant to. The Holy Mother is my witness. I just hit him. He came to take my horses away. I had two horses, such good horses they were. I saved and I got into debt to buy them, but the men came to take them away. I must have hit harder than I had intended. I just saw red. It's an awful thing to see red. I know I've committed a mortal sin. It's right that I should die. But I can't stand waiting like this. It's such a waste. If they would only let me plant my crops. I should be working now, in the fields. I wouldn't run away. If they can't make up their minds when to punish me, why don't they let me out to work? I ask you? I wouldn't run away. It's just the waste . . ." He folded his hands and started to pray again.

"And you?" Charles asked the old man.

"He's a tramp," said the boy. "They picked him up two months ago. He's been picked up for tramping several times. He can't help it."

Now the old man spoke, but even when he talked he went on singing.

"Nature is so beautiful," came out of him in his tuneless whisper, "why should I stay at home, under a roof, locked in, when I can have the stars shining on me at night and the sun to lead me through the day? It makes me sick to be in a house, between walls, stones. I love the roads, the wide big ones and the little paths among the fields . . ."

Charles stopped listening. I am in here for resisting arrest, he thought. I might be left here for months to come, waiting. How do I know? If it's true what these people say, I may be waiting trial here for a year.

But I can't wait for a year. I've got to try to get out. I've got things to do. They can't punish me for resisting arrest . . . they can't! Because you can't make a crazy man responsible for his actions. They will have to send me back to the asylum. They have my papers. They know where I came from. They know that I was released only a few days ago. They will send me back. They'll have to send me back to the Casa della Pace!

For a second a smile flickered across his face as he followed up the thoughts which had begun to take shape in his mind while the plain clothes men had been pushing him into the car. Everything was lost, then suddenly, nothing was lost! They have arrested me as Vittorio da Ponte, and Vittorio da Ponte can't be held responsible for what he does because he has been in an asylum for twenty-four years and he can prove it. All that matters now is that they don't forget me, that among their many prisoners they get around to Vittorio da Ponte, quick! So that they may send him back where he belongs . . .

They must not be allowed to forget me.

"And you?" asked the boy. "You don't look like one of us. You . . . you sort of look like a gentleman."

Charles put his fingers to his lips. "Hush," he said, and, putting his mouth close to the boy's large, dirty ear, he whispered, "You see, everybody thinks I am insane . . . but I am not . . . I am really not crazy . . . it's just that nobody will believe me, so I run away." And he forced himself to laugh, to laugh loud and high, false, unnatural laughter which echoed back from the walls.

The boy moved uneasily. Charles saw him pull the peasant's sleeve, saw him whisper something to him. The peasant looked at him, sudden horror in his eyes. Charles went on laughing. The peasant now said something to the old tramp. He couldn't hear what it was, but the tramp only shrugged his shoulders. "There are many strange birds in God's wide world," he sang.

A guard could be heard coming down the long,

narrow corridor outside, his heavy boots and big keys making an uncanny and imposing sound. All of them sat breathless, their bodies stiff, their faces turned unconsciously towards the door, their senses alert. In front of the heavy iron door the steps stopped. The small window in its upper part was opened. They could see two bright dark eyes looking into the cell. Then a voice called "Da Ponte."

Charles, still laughing, got up. The door was opened. Two armed guards stood outside and took him between them.

CHAPTER VII

WHILE he was being marched off, Charles kept telling himself with every step he took: Remember – you're Vittorio da Ponte. Charles Barrett is dead. You never knew him. Or, if there ever was a Charles Barrett – he was a young boy who was taken prisoner during the last war and was killed while trying to escape. Remember that. Remember what Dr. Pederazzini told you. He didn't tell you all those things for nothing. He wanted you to believe them. Charles Barrett is dead. Therefore nobody can arrest him. They've arrested Vittorio da Ponte because, on a routine raid, he made himself suspicious by resisting. You have nothing to fear. No judge would condemn a man who has been confined for twenty-four years. He said it over and over again in his mind. He told every vein, every blood vessel in his body: Remember – you are Vittorio da Ponte. And that's your only chance.

They had reached the top floor of the building. At the end of the long corridor he could see a door open. They marched him through it into a sort of anteroom where several clerks behind a low wooden railing sat writing. All of them looked up and one of them reached for the telephone.

"The prisoner da Ponte is here." And then, turning to Charles and his escort, "You can go right in."

The door to the adjoining room swung open and Charles could see that it was upholstered in heavy brown leather to numb any sound which might carry through ordinary wood. Suddenly he grew quite calm; he felt almost relieved that, contrary to his expectations, he was being given a hearing right away. All that remained for him to do now, since he had not been forgotten among the hundreds of prisoners, was to act in a way that would make everyone believe that his mind had snapped again the moment the police had come for him.

The room which he entered was of ordinary shape and size. Several steel file cases stood along the walls, between them a leather couch, two chairs at a small table, a cuspidor conveniently near. Between the two large deep windows sat a man behind an office writing desk, at his left a stenographer. Behind them hung two large framed photographs, already a little faded. One showed Mussolini as he might have looked years before:

less fat, his face not yet bloated, his heavy jaw jutting forward; the other, the gentle old features of the little King. "For country, King and Mussolini!" the crowds had cried in those days. Some had joined the movement because they were patriots and thought it might help Italy, others because they were told it was for the King, and they loved the little King or what he stood for and were loyal to the crown, and the rest had thrown in their lot because they believed in the new man. And then a small snowflake had grown into an avalanche and had swept over them all.

Through one of the windows, the one that stood open, he could see the cupola of the Pantheon, and far away, on one of the hills at the right side of the Tiber, the outlines of the church of San Pietro in Montorio. He knew where he was. In the old *questura* of the Via Collegio Romano.

Suddenly the man behind the desk moved. He rose and sat down again quickly. The guards stepped back to the door and remained standing there.

"Come closer," said the man.

Charles went up to the desk.

The man, apparently a high police official, wore the black shirt of the Fascists. A startling amount of colored ribbons and medals decorated his chest. He seemed very proud of them because his hand went up to them and played with them, as a woman plays with a string of pearls to attract attention to her fine new jewelry, trying to impress others with it. His face was common but handsome in a cheap way, with a little mustache above a weak, vain mouth and a straight little nose, its nostrils moving all the time, either out of bad habit or indicating passion. Charles didn't like his eyes. They were bright, almost completely round, like little black buttons, and they bulged slightly like the eyes sewn on a rag doll. He couldn't have been much older than Charles, maybe about thirty-five or six.

The man eyed him just as intently for a while, taking in Charles's whole appearance as if this first impression he was forming of the prisoner was going to decide his opinion.

On the desk Charles could see his wallet and all his papers spread out and a closed blue folder which apparently held his case history. So. He knows where I have been all these years, he thought. He knows that I have been confined.

His glance wandered out of the window again. He couldn't resist that view. I wish I were over there, he thought, on the hill. You can see all of Rome from there, better, almost, than from any other point.

He expected ordinary questioning – name,

birth, and so on – but when the man finally made up his mind to address him again, he started. In a sharp, high voice, the man said, "Confess that you are guilty!"

Charles didn't answer right away. Think before you answer, he told himself. The man knows who you are. He skips all preliminaries. He might even be thinking what you want him to think, that you suffered a relapse.

"I . . . I . . ." he began, and paused. Then, forcing his voice to sound unnatural, "I don't know what you mean."

The man looked at him, his glance fixed on the prisoner's chin. "So. You don't know what I mean."

Charles didn't say anything. Keep your face blank, Vittorio da Ponte. You don't understand a thing. You have no idea what all this is about.

"Well. Then tell me where you were Tuesday night."

Make him speak. Why? . . . He shrugged his shoulders and remained silent.

"You were at the Excelsior!" the man barked at him.

Charles nodded. "The Excelsior. Yes. I was at the Excelsior."

"And where were you before that?"

He pretended that his memory had come back to him. "I sat at the Fontana di Trevi."

"At the Fontana di Trevi. And what did you do there?"

"I watched the people. I like the people. I always watch the people."

"You didn't meet anyone there, did you? You didn't have an appointment there?"

"I just watched the people," Charles said.

"And then you went to the Excelsior."

"I went to the Excelsior," Charles repeated after him. . . . (Make sense, but not too much sense.)

"And what did you do at the Excelsior?"

"I had a drink."

"You had a drink. And then?"

"Then I went home."

"You went home. You went to bed."

"I went to bed."

"You are lying! You didn't go to bed."

Charles seemed to remember. "That's right. I didn't go to bed. I didn't undress. I just lay down on the bed."

Why wasn't he being asked if he pleaded guilty of having knocked several people about? Why no question of his resisting arrest?

"And why didn't you undress?"

"I was not sleepy."

"And why weren't you sleepy? Why didn't you undress?"

"I don't know."

"You didn't expect somebody? You weren't waiting for something, were you?"

"I wasn't waiting for anything. I wasn't sleepy so I didn't undress."

"And then my officers came. Did you expect them?"

"I was most surprised," said Charles. "Most surprised, indeed."

Feel your way, he warned himself. What is he after? He doesn't want you to plead guilty of resisting arrest. Keep that in mind. For God's sake, keep that in mind!

The man's voice changed. It sounded ironical now, biting. His eyes glittered. "Not so surprised as not to be able to collect your wits instantly and knock them out!"

"They gave me a shock," Charles said. He was whispering now.

"A shock. So you hadn't expected them."

Charles shook his head violently. "No. Oh, no! I hadn't expected them."

He could feel his heart pounding in his throat.

Again the man changed his voice. It sounded softer now, almost gentle. He was a grand little actor, this little man. "You'd better confess," he said. "I'm telling you, it would be much better for you to confess."

Charles's heart missed a beat. All this had nothing to do with his having knocked out the policeman, the S.S. guards, with fleeing from . . . This man wanted something from him, he was trying to make him say something . . .

The man went on speaking, very softly. "We can understand that there are some people who don't care for the Germans. Just tell us who gave you the order to place the bomb in the Excelsior. Tell us the name, and things will be easier for you. It isn't so difficult to remember the name of the man who told you – or is it? Are you aware that a crime like this is punishable with death?"

He paused to see what impression his words were making on the prisoner.

(Keep your face calm. Stop your hands from trembling. This looks bad . . . But keep right on acting. Don't lose your nerve. That's what he's after. He wants to find that man. He must find him at any price.)

"Yes. Punishable by death," the man repeated. "But perhaps we won't shoot you if you tell us the name. Don't you see how bad your position is? You will be condemned to death in any event. But if you name the man . . ." He left the sentence hanging in midair, the indication of a promise which he had not made, and went on, "You see, we don't believe that you made the bomb. We think it was given to you."

"Bomb?" said Charles, as if he had only now grasped the sense of what was being said. "Bomb? I never planted any bomb! No! No! I've never even seen a bomb! I . . . I don't hate the Germans. I . . . I like them!"

For a second the man behind the desk seemed shaken.

"So, you like the Germans," he said then, and a bit of surprise still lingered in his voice.

"They are efficient," said Charles, quickly now, almost enthusiastically. "They are smart. They're helping us win the war. Don't you agree with me?"

This time the man eyed him from the side, the cautious glance of a child who thinks his leg is being pulled. Then he pulled himself together. "So. You insist on not telling me the truth." He paused. His next question exploded like a shot. "Why then did you run away when my officers came for you?"

Charles caught his breath. "I . . ." he said, mastering his voice. "I didn't run away."

"You didn't run away."

"I didn't run away. I went for a walk on the Corso."

Suddenly his broken thumb began to hurt.

Charles was glad. He put his whole hand across his thumb, pressing it hard, increasing the pain. This will help, he thought, to keep my mind clear.

"Oh. You took a little promenade on the Corso. And where did you sleep? Where did you sleep?"

"I slept in my bed," said Charles quietly.

"And where is your bed?"

(Careful, now. Be very careful. Don't mention the Casa della Pace, or he'll think you're driving to that point, that you're not so crazy as to have forgotten that you're crazy.)

"My bed?" he said. "My bed is in a large wide room. In Verona. In a big house. My father slept in it . . . my grandfather . . . my great-grandfather . . . my great-great-grandfather . . . It has always been in my family. Always! Don't you know that?" And, almost hysterical now . . . (God! Make my voice hysterical!): "My father will come and get me! He won't allow you to question me like this! My father is a Senator! The King loves him! He is a friend of the King. He will come and call for me."

The man's voice sounded gentle now, with a trace of pity in it. "Calm yourself, da Ponte. Calm yourself."

The man is acting, Charles realized. He is acting just as much as I am. I want him to believe my act. He wants me to believe that I planted the bomb.

"Calm yourself. And now listen to me. You only have to admit that you planted the bomb. Come now, calm down. Everything will be all right if you confess."

The pain in his thumb. Thank heaven for the pain! . . . Remember the day Joe swung the baseball bat against your hand and you couldn't play for almost two months?

"Oh, yes. I confess. I did hit one man over the head with the water bottle. But he came to kill me. I had to defend myself."

The man spoke sharply again. "We are not talking about the man you hit. We are talking about the bomb. Now. Try to remember. Somebody gave you the bomb, wanted you to place it at the hotel because he didn't like the Germans."

"But I love the Germans!"

Charles grew suddenly aware of the man who was sitting quietly on a straight chair next to the desk, a stenoblock on his lap, his pencil moving quickly between his fingers. He looked at him. The man had no face. To Charles it looked like a carrot, long and thin, with a gray beard for roots, flat and wide on the top, with a shock of unkempt hair standing up for its sprouting little leaves.

His inquisitor was speaking with great warmth now, as if he were really trying to do his best for the prisoner, as a doctor would speak to a stubborn child that won't take its medicine. "Pay attention now to what I say, da Ponte. You are going to be condemned to death in any case, because your resistance and your flight are proof enough of your guilt. But if you confess that you planted the bomb, I will recommend you to the clemency of His Royal Majesty, the King, and by that you may be allowed to live."

Charles lifted his head to where the portrait of the little King hung. He would never be recommended for clemency. The King would never hear about him . . . and he, Charles, would be told in a regretful voice that the King had seen fit not to exercise mercy. . . .

He looked away again quickly, and his eyes wandered to the window. Ah, to stand now on the hill he could see so far away. He shook his head violently. "No. I didn't do it. I didn't do it."

Behind his desk the man rose, his left hand clutching several of the medals on his chest as if he had to hang on to them and what they stood for. "You will regret not having confessed," he said, and now his voice was angry.

His little mustache trembled in badly concealed temper and with a wide, sweeping gesture which he had taken the trouble to learn to imitate, he said, "Guards – take him away."

He was led back to the cell where the old tramp, the sturdy peasant and the slender, big-eyed boy viewed him with curiosity, surprised to see him again.

"I didn't think you'd come back," the boy said. And it sounded as if he had hoped not to be forced to share a cell with a man who had broken loose from an asylum.

"Why, there you are again!" said the peasant. "And I was envying you for getting a hearing so quickly. Now you will have to wait for your trial."

There won't be any trial, thought Charles.

The tramp turned his face to him. "Did you see the sky? The sun? A bird?" His watery old eyes were filled with such longing that it made Charles grit his teeth. "The trees must have little leaves now, tiny little leaves. Makes the treetops look like green veils. The camellias should be out . . . red, and pink, and white. And the wind, ah, the wind of the spring coming across the sea. Sometimes even here, when I lie awake at night and I am lucky I can hear the wind sing. It gets caught in the big buildings, but it can get out again. No city can stop it. It can blow and blow over hills and meadows, over fields and lakes."

Charles was suddenly very tired. He dropped to the floor, onto the dirty straw through which the damp cold penetrated as if it were nothing better than paper. He crossed his arms behind his neck and rested his head on them. But as soon as he lay outstretched and the blood began to flow evenly through his veins, he knew that sleep had deserted him, that what he had felt was nothing but dreadful mental weariness. He let his lids fall over his eyes and pretended to be asleep.

"If only I hadn't hit the men!" he kept thinking. "If only I hadn't run . . . If I just hadn't lost my nerve! No. No, Charles, that isn't it. As long as there was a raid, they would have taken you. . . . They needed a scapegoat . . . that was what the man who cross-examined you was after. He wasn't interested in two S.S. guards and an Italian officer whom you knocked down, nor in the other man who came up the stairs when you thought the way was clear. He is interested in only one thing — in finding that criminal who left the bomb at the Excelsior. He hasn't found him yet. Among all the suspicious people they must have arrested during last night and today, they haven't found the one they are looking for. If they don't find him soon, the man will lose his job. He must find the criminal. The Germans, their agents, their S.S. have told him that the man must be found – at any price. Not in a month's time, not in a week's time, but now! Maybe they even threatened the Italians with more Gestapo men in Italian positions if the Italian police is so inefficient as not to be able to . . .

The man, he knew clearly, had had his attention fixed on him because he had resisted arrest and fled, but – the moment he had seen his papers, had seen Vittorio da Ponte's release from the Casa della Pace, an idea had formed in the man's mind. Here was his victim! A crazy man whom he could perhaps talk into a confession. And come out with all the credit attached to such quick and smart work – finding the criminal within twenty-four hours!

Charles tried to adjust his mind to what could be going on in a mind like the one the man must have. He tried to put himself in the man's place. He couldn't. Forget Charles Barrett, he told himself. Think of it as Vittorio da Ponte. He couldn't. He had grown up in a country where law and order were respected and justice was held high, where the innocent would be acquitted after a fair trial, where one had to prove another man's guilt before condemning him. For the first time in his life, Charles J. Barrett from Tulsa, Oklahoma, could feel what people forced to live in a Fascistic country must feel like. That isn't living, he thought. That's walking along an abyss, week after week, day after day, hour after hour, walking on a tightrope across an abyss into which law and justice and the common right of the common man have been pushed. . . . For the first time he felt the terror of those people who faced arbitrary rule. Injustice, in place of what they had a right to expect as citizens — the law.

A country without law is doomed, he thought, a country where law ceases to exist, and where instead every evil instinct inherent in human nature is licensed in the name of law and order, can only breed criminals!

Oh, snap out of it! he told himself impatiently. What help are philosophical thoughts now? You knew all that. This is what you came over here to fight in the first place, this very thing. You just hadn't ever felt its impact before. You knew it existed, the way you know a shortage of bread exists — but you just never felt hunger before. Snap out of it now! You're in a hell of a spot and you know it. You won't get out of here and you know it. You came along, the most convenient victim those people could find to hang their bomb onto, a man who isn't responsible for his actions. What a beautiful solution! No bad feeling can grow from it between the Germans and Italians. For once the Italian police has outsmarted the

Gestapo. They can't create an issue. They can't do a thing. Everything's perfectly clear and above-board! There is no antagonistic feeling between Italians and Germans, none whatsoever! You see, Himmler, it was a crazy man who planted that bomb, to blow up the Excelsior with all its German officers and S.S. men and Gestapo agents. Everybody is going to be perfectly happy!

And how had it come to pass that Charles Barrett, American, was making them so happy?

He sat up with a start. Had he been figuring everything all wrong? Had he been on the wrong track all the time? Was Pietro's story about the Contessa and a list of important people willing to end the war just a mere accident, just a story created by his crazy mind? Had he, Charles Barrett, not been sent to the Casa della Pace for the reasons he had thought out — to find the Contessa and the list — but for another purpose? For the purpose of making the most delightful scapegoat for something that had been planned to happen just during the days he was to be in Rome? Someone who would not create an issue . . . A loony . . .

"I hope he isn't getting one of his fits," he heard the boy say. "Look at him. He looks wild."

So he had frightened the kid, and the kid believed that he was crazy. He lay back again. He was utterly confused now. . . . I'll probably never find out, he thought. There will be a trial, a short trial, and some German officers will be present because this is an occasion that calls for them. There will be a debate, maybe, as to whether they should show mercy and send me back to the Casa della Pace; but if the Germans feel like their compatriot who came out to inspect the asylum, they will shoot me regardless. . . .

The old tramp suddenly knelt down beside him. "This isn't nice to lie on," he said. "But I close my eyes and tell myself that this is a soft, green meadow with little daisies and forget-me-nots, or a sweet-smelling haystack, or the elastic ground of a wood strewn with pine-needles, like the woods around Pisa . . . such a lot of beautiful pines . . . and then, and when I am sleepy, I can fool myself. But when I wake up, I know it is only the hard cement floor of a prison."

He lay down and pulled one of the blankets over his body. "I miss my dog so much," he said. "He was an old dog, but he liked the life we led. Sometimes we went hungry, but he didn't mind. The guard told me the little one followed me up to the *questura* and sat outside for three days, waiting for me to come out, and then they drove him away. I wonder where he is now."

He was crying softly, the tears streaming down

his face, big single drops. "I hope you don't mind, *amico,*" he sang. "You see, when one is very old, one isn't any more ashamed of one's tears."

Charles touched the man's small, bony shoulder almost in a caress. The old tramp smiled at him and winked a wet eye.

"You know," he said, his voice scarcely audible now. "One day I'll break out and find myself a little place by a stream, the water floating gently and the clouds sailing along the sky and a big chestnut tree giving shade, and there I'll sit and wait for death. I'm not going to die here." He closed his eyes and within a minute was asleep, with the quick sleep that comes easily to very old people.

Die, thought Charles. . . .

"*In any case you will be condemned to death,*" the man's voice rang out. . . . Die? Did I ever think of dying when I volunteered? Sure, I did. But that was something else. That was fate and all of us had the same chance of coming back, of living, or dying – in battle, the honorable death of a soldier.

The peasant stretched out on his other side. "You get tired of sitting around like this with nothing to do, don't you? It's funny – but you never get half so exhausted when you work. You keep the things going that in return keep you going

— that's what matters most, isn't it?" He shook his head anxiously. "The asparagus," he said. "They should be coming up now, the west fields first . . . I wonder . . ." He was praying again. "One should get a good price for them nowadays," he added after he had finished his rosary.

The little boy got up, bent to pick up the blanket and rolled it up, putting it on the stone bench where he lay down, evidently preferring that hard bed to Charles's immediate neighborhood. After a little while, when the small cell was filled with the snoring of the peasant and the little sigh the tramp made in his sleep, the boy turned toward Charles and spoke softly. "You'd better go to sleep," he said. "You see, they feed us only twice a day, once early in the morning and once about noon. You missed that. You came in too late for it. In the evening there's just water." He pointed with his chin to the table. The pitcher had been filled while Charles had been away. The boy's hand moved in the direction of the door. A pail had been placed there to serve as a toilet.

Charles whispered, "Don't they ever take us out?"

"Once in a while, when they get around to it," the boy said. "There are so many, you see. They don't always have time to take us out for half an hour." He stopped. But after a little while during which he seemed to be dreaming with eyes wide open, he said in a small voice, apparently having forgotten what Charles had told him about himself, or just not caring any longer in his loneliness: "Tell me. You are so much older than I, you should have so much more experience – do girls forget easily?"

"No," said Charles. "Was she pretty?"

"The prettiest one in the whole village, straight as a sunflower, with lips like a little cherry and eyes as big as marbles and beautiful long black hair and . . . and a vicious temper. She said she would kill me if she ever found me with another girl." He smiled, lost in his memories. "Mind if I talk? You see, the old one, *il vecchio,* he doesn't know any more what love can mean, and the other one, he just cares for manure and vegetables and rain and his horses and cows and goats. He must be quite a rich man. They don't really love any longer. They love only what they possess. But I am young and poor. I was a fisherman. She used to wait for me at the beach when I came home. My boat had a little red sail and I knew the waters well . . ."

He went on for a long time, sometimes hard to follow, for he spoke in his native Sicilian dialect; but then, finally, with the simple politeness of his race, he asked, "And you . . . did you have a girl?"

"Yes," said Charles. "I had a girl."

"Don't want to talk about her?"

Charles shook his head.

The boy waited for a while, then he said "Good night," and turned around, his little muscular bottom rounded in his tight trousers.

Outside the high window it had grown completely dark. What time could it be? Eight o'clock? Nine? He couldn't tell. . . . Sybilla, he thought. Does she know what has happened to me? She will have called the Pension Elvira. Someone will have told her. But perhaps they are ashamed to mention what happened at the Elvira and won't say a word. Then she will go there. She will find out. Oh, she would find out through the papers. But maybe they don't print the news here. Maybe editors can't publish what they know, that a suspect has been caught who apparently is the culprit. Anyhow, they won't mention names.

He recalled the day in the library when he had tried to check up on Pietro Vantoni. He had come across a great many items — political murders, sabotage — but names had rarely been mentioned. . . . She will find out, he thought again. But what can she do? Nothing. If only I had told her the name of the Casa della Pace and Pederazzini's name! She could get in touch with them, get him here, get him to testify. . . . Oh, no, Charles. If you are right in assuming that Pietro's story was a mere story and that you have been planted here as a scapegoat for what certain conspirators planned . . . then Pederazzini would not come to your assistance.

All I can do now, he thought, is to tell that man, or if I don't get a chance to talk to him again, to tell the judge, that I am not Vittorio da Ponte, have never been crazy, that I am really Charles J. Barrett, from Tulsa, Oklahoma, and to check up in their receiving camp for prisoners. That's my only chance.

A guard opened the door, came in, flashed his light from one to the other. "Come on," he said to Charles. "I have to put you in a single cell."

"Why?" He hadn't meant to ask.

The guard shrugged his shoulders. "You should know," he said, not unkindly. "We always do that."

And by this Charles knew that it was too late to tell the truth, that it wouldn't help him any longer to confess his true personality, because they wouldn't believe him, because they would not choose to believe him. But they can't shoot Vittorio da Ponte, he kept saying to himself, as he tried to feel his way about in his lonely little cell. Vittorio da Ponte can't be held responsible!

But they will, the walls seemed to echo back. *Because in a dictatorship they can do whatever seems most opportune to them . . .*

It was shortly past eight the next morning when Sybilla finally managed to see the high official of the police, the same man who had examined Charles.

"Good morning, Signor Bartoldi," she said, seating herself in the chair he pushed at a more convenient angle for her. "I am sorry to disturb you as early as this, but the matter is of great importance."

"I'll be very glad to do whatever I can for you, Contessina," Bartoldi answered, this time playing the charming gentleman he had so often read about. He could not very well have done anything but receive her. After all, she was a member of the aristocracy, her connections reached into the highest circles. Maybe the circles were not as powerful as his own, but they certainly counted and could make a lot of trouble if they wanted to.

"You are holding a man I am very much interested in," Sybilla said, and she snapped her cigaret case open and offered him one. "A man by the name of Vittorio da Ponte, a very good friend of mine. I understand he is being held in connection with the Excelsior affair."

He pretended to think for a while before he remembered. "Yes. We do have a man here by that name; but, may I add I think you must be mistaken? He couldn't possibly be a friend of yours."

"Why not?" said Sybilla, and looked at her hands as if she were bored. "You mean because he's crazy?"

Bartoldi sat back in his chair. He blew out the smoke of the cigaret in perfect little circles. "How do you happen to know that I am holding the man?" he said. "The matter has been treated with the utmost secrecy."

"Never mind that," she said haughtily, but smiling. "It should be enough for you to know that friends, mutual friends of yours and mine, told me."

The man thought rapidly. If she knew it from the people he had notified, she most certainly also had access to that powerful group.

"The man is innocent," Sybilla went on. "I would vouch for him any time. You see, his father was a very dear friend of my uncle Arturo, Conte Rossi. He died fighting for Italy in the last war. His young son, Vittorio, volunteered, and as a consequence of the war, and some head wounds, went out of his mind."

"That's all in the record," the man said.

"He's only been released recently."

"I saw his release from the Casa della Pace."

Casa della Pace, thought Sybilla, Casa della Pace. And she smiled.

"I have come here in case you would like . . ." She began, stopped, and started again. "I thought the poor man must most certainly have suffered greatly through all this excitement. I wouldn't like him to be sent back to the Casa della Pace all by himself. I thought he might like to see a face he knows, someone he trusts. So my uncle and I have come to go with him as soon as you release him. Conte Rossi is waiting outside. We will wait for him."

"Contessina," said Bartoldi. "I am sorry. I don't think it would be a good idea to wait for him."

She looked at him, her eyes open wide.

"Because, you see," Bartoldi said slowly, "I am afraid I'm not going to release him."

"You're not going to release him? Not going to send him back to the asylum? But you must! You should get in touch with his doctor out there, the man who has been treating him for almost twenty-five years. What are you holding him for? He's crazy!"

"You can't say that. He has been released as cured," said Bartoldi slowly. There was the flicker of a smile in his eyes.

"But he has not committed a crime!"

"How do you know that?"

"I told you I was ready to vouch for him."

"The trial will prove whether he is guilty or not."

"The trial! What trial? A man who is innocent can't be put on trial! That's impossible!"

"Contessina," he said, "during the last few years many things have happened we would never have dreamed of. The Germans insist it is their matter because it happened at the Excelsior and because a German saw him leave the hotel and walk over to the Pension Elvira, and put us on his track."

"If you let him stand trial," Sybilla said, "the Germans will shoot him. They . . ."

Bartoldi shrugged his shoulders and, to pay back for the cigaret, took a box of candy out of his writing desk and offered her a chocolate. "That, Contessina, is beyond my power," he said. "If the Germans feel they want to shoot a man, I can't stop them."

"You don't have to send him up for trial," she said. "That's where they can't stop you. If you release him now and have him sent back to the Casa della Pace, they couldn't do a thing! They could only keep on trying to find the real criminal!"

To this Bartoldi didn't answer.

Yes, he thought, you are right. The Germans would keep on poking their noses into my affairs, they would take over more and more positions, assume more and more responsibility, they would push me more and more aside. They would, if I let this man be sent back to the asylum, most certainly insist on our finding the criminal; they wouldn't rest till they got him. Why, this is so beautifully simple! he thought. There is enough evidence to condemn him. . . . He was at the Excelsior, he didn't go to bed, he knocked the men out who came for him. . . . He fled, he hid. . . . Enough evidence to close this case once and for all and keep them out of my office. It's their business to decide whether they think he was sane when he committed the crime or not. . . .

"You can't do it," said Sybilla. "It just isn't done!"

"I'm really very sorry," he said, with exquisite politeness. "I regret extremely, but I don't think I can help you in this matter." After all, he reflected, she couldn't know too powerful people. If she did, she wouldn't have come, they would just have phoned him orders. He rose and saw her to the door. "*Arrivederci,*" he said, and bowed.

He locked the door after her and went over to a small door that led into a cabinet. There he looked at himself in the mirror, straightened out his tie mechanically — he was very satisfied with himself. The Germans would be satisfied also . . . such a beautifully simple case! They would jump at the chance of having a crazy man for the victim. No issue. No stink would be raised, and he would stay in office.

In front of the *questura,* the cab was waiting. Uncle Arturo climbed out when he saw Sybilla coming and helped her in. He didn't ask any questions. Her pale face, her set jaw, told him everything. The cab drove quickly, up the Via Vittorio Veneto, and turned into the Porta Pinciana, taking the short cut through the Giardini Borghese. It drove past the marble statues and busts of former great men, when Uncle Arturo couldn't contain himself any longer. "It's impossible!" he said in an agitated voice. "It just can't happen! He is the son of a man who was a friend of mine, a man who fell fighting for his country!"

Sybilla looked at the old man who didn't know anything about the true personality of Vittorio da Ponte.

"He is going to turn him over to the Germans," she said. Her voice was dead.

"It's against all the principles of civilization and humanity!" Uncle Arturo said.

She didn't answer. She kept looking straight ahead, the only way she knew of to keep herself sitting upright.

"We must make an appeal," he went on. "As soon as we get home, I will write to His Majesty the King. His father was a friend of mine. I am not going to let this happen!"

She moved her hand and put it across his trembling knee. "It will be too late," she said.

She thought of the hour of dusk, when he and she had sat together on the floor of her room and the pigeon had cooed outside the window. She had been able to put her head on his shoulder and cry. . . .

The cab stopped in front of the house in the Via Raimondi. She didn't wait for the driver to be paid. She went straight in and up the stairs into her room. The room was the same . . . but the man she could have trusted with her entire life was gone.

"What can I do?" she asked herself, aloud. "What can I do?"

Into her memory came the past hours of yesterday – the news in the paper which she had at first in no way connected with him; Silvio giving her the message that he had called . . . And when she had called back, the excited maid telling her what had happened to the nice Signor da Ponte on Floor 3, and being suddenly interrupted by the shrill voice of a woman who later turned out to be the owner of the Pension Elvira . . . The way she had racked her brain after she had gone to the pension to find out for herself what had happened, why and how he could have called her during lunchtime, and then not let her hear anything, trying to piece things together. Naturally, he must have thought that the police had found out, and fled, then called her to make sure that there was no connection between his planned arrest and her security. And then, the notice in the paper, that the culprit had been arrested at one o'clock . . . no name . . . his call had come through at twenty minutes to one . . . the frantic evening she had spent till Uncle Arturo had finally thought of a former Commissioner of Police whom he knew, who promised to find out what he could. And, late that night, the report . . . they were holding a man at the *questura* by the name of Vittorio da Ponte. The former Commissioner couldn't do a thing. . . . Sorry, but, perhaps, if Sybilla were to go herself and see Bartoldi . . . Yes, Commissioner Bartoldi, the most important man now. And she had tried to bluff her way through and had failed. . . .

"Hush, baby, hush . . ." Her mother had said that: "Hush, my baby," and had caressed her with gentle hands. Her mother . . . she had known so many important people. . . .

"Look through her diaries, her notebooks, her engagement books," his voice seemed to whisper through the room. "Write all the names down . . . the people she has seen, during the last year, let's say . . ." In the excitement of yesterday she hadn't found time to do it. . . .

She walked across the floor and into her mother's suite, which she had not entered since the Contessa Luisa San Vigilio had been buried. She didn't look about her now, she didn't even pull aside the heavy yellow curtains; she switched on the electric light and walked across the soft carpets into the small living room next to the dressing room, where her mother had used to read and write. There, in the corner, between wall and window, stood her writing desk . . . an Early American mahogany desk—looking alien between the heavily carved ceiling and door. But Mother had insisted on bringing these things over from the United States, a little bit of America in an old Renaissance house. On the shelf, her collection of little red and blue lamps, of amber glass. A Boston rocker in the corner, the white porcelain poodle for a doorstop – I have no time to be sad now, Sybilla said to herself.

She sat down and opened the desk. Someone must have forgotten a box of cards here, cards which they had sent out to their closest friends instead of putting the notice of the Contessa's death in the paper. Probably Tina, looking up addresses to see if someone had been forgotten, or making sure she had the envelope addressed right . . .

Sybilla pushed it aside. Here, in the left hand drawer, a diary. Almost empty except for some hastily scribbled notes on a few pages. "The prices on the black market – terrific! Wonder what's going on at home – How do the Americans feel about this country now? They will have to fight it, naturally; but do they really consider us enemies?" Mother, darling! "At home" and "us" in the same line. . . . "I couldn't bear to see this country destroyed . . . the people are all right . . . indifferent, yes . . . but how long have we been indifferent at home? Wish I could be back there . . . the Villa Borghese and Central Park . . . what makes the real difference is not atmosphere or culture or beauty, but love. Poor Augusto . . . he knows I'm suffering . . . I know he is because he knows that now, when there is war, I feel I belong . . ."

More notes like these. . . . How strangely alive the handwriting looks. Perhaps he has written me a letter, the night I couldn't see him at the Fontana di Trevi . . . maybe he went home and sat down and told me, "Sybilla, baby . . . *bambina* . . ." The police are holding it now if he wrote it. But one day they may send it on to me and the writing will look as if he were still alive. But he will be dead, buried somewhere . . . Where do the Germans bury the people they shoot?

Another note caught her glance. "Have to give up seeing those most dear to my heart, those who could understand what I feel and hope for. . . . I would only add to their difficulties. I mustn't compromise them through my presence. Life is doubly hard, right at this moment, when American troops have landed in Africa. Lucky Billa. She is so young. She doesn't yet realize what it means. She will never know. She is too young to understand. . . ."

Sybilla leaned back. She was crying, but she didn't know it. In this very room she had sat only three weeks ago. "What are you reading, *cara?*" she had asked. "Aren't you going out tonight? There is a big reception after the opera." And her mother had answered, "I have seen all the operas in my life that I want to see." "But I thought you loved 'Aïda'?" "I prefer to read. You go, *bambina.* Make yourself look pretty . . ."

So Mother had been afraid of compromising her friends. She had always hated to embarrass people. "What are you reading?" "Oh, just a book about San Francisco." Luisa San Vigilio had come from San Francisco. How homesick she must have been to read little novels just because in them somebody described the Golden Gate and the Oakland Bridge and the Marin County hills! . . .

Sybilla reached for her mother's engagement book. How sick with longing he must be – he who had so unwillingly let himself be drawn into a conspiracy of which she knew nothing . . .

Names, names, names. None of them important. None of these names could help her. Where were the names and addresses of those people who mattered, whom her mother had known before Italy and America had declared war?

Sybilla put her head on her arms and began to sob softly.

Uncle Arturo's voice called up from downstairs. "Where are you?"

She went to the door and answered him. After a little while, she heard his steps approaching the room. How old those steps sounded, how tired; how sweet he was to bother at all, out of sheer decency, just because he couldn't bear injustice!

Instead of withdrawing into the shelter of old age, he took any amount of trouble. . . .

"Oh, here you are!" he said. "What are you doing in here?"

She sighed. "I'd sort of hoped to find a name among Mother's papers, a name of a friend of hers who is influential and could help. . . . But Mother seems to have broken off all connections with important people. She seems to have been completely out of touch with anyone who matters. . . ."

"Yes," said Uncle Arturo. "She broke off with her best friends — but I remember them. Some of them. Just let me think now. . . . Whom did she see very often before all this dreadful trouble began?"

CHAPTER VIII

UNCLE ARTURO crossed his arms behind his back and began to walk the room with his carefully measured steps. In his old, pedantic way he began to name names, going back into the histories of several families. But though his voice was quiet and the movement of his body calm, he was aroused and excited. Again and again he would repeat, "His father was a friend of mine. He died fighting. . . . Bartoldi knows the boy is mentally ill. He can't turn him over!"

Sybilla hardly said a word. Now and then she would shake her head, at the mention of a name, because the man her uncle mentioned had grown unpopular and no longer possessed any influence. Then, from downstairs, she heard the front door being opened. For a second her heart leapt with a sudden, desperate hope — that Bartoldi had changed his mind and was sending a message to her. She didn't know that she was running when she passed Uncle Arturo and flew out into the corridor and towards the stairs. Silvio was coming up, carrying a little silver tray. "What is it?" she said impatiently, breathlessly. Then she saw the small, white visiting card.

"BARONE CLAUDIO TORLANI," she read.

Her heart fell. . . . Not now, she thought. Oh, not now, when I have no time to spare.

She walked back into the room and said, "Torlani is downstairs. Could you see him for me, please?"

Uncle Arturo took the card from her trembling fingers and repeated the name. "I am afraid not, *carina,*" he said softly. "He probably came to pay his respects and condolences to you."

"Where do you want to receive the *Signore,* Contessina?" asked Silvio, who had followed her. "The *salotto?* Or should I lead the *Signore* into the library?"

Oh, not the library, not the *salotto!* He might stay longer than was absolutely necessary. It was rude to receive him in the hall, she knew. Yet time was so precious.

"Think of someone," she said desperately to her uncle – "of a minister we could approach. No. Stay here. Don't come down. I am coming, Silvio." The servant stepped back to let her go first.

Downstairs in the wide chilly hall where she had first met Vittorio da Ponte, she saw Claudio Torlani walking up and down. He was a tall, splendidly bred man. He had been an Admiral already in the last war and now he was in command again. Once he had been one of her mother's many admirers, but in the last few years she had seen him only on big, official occasions. . . . He has aged, she thought. His hair was silver-gray above his tanned face.

He turned when he heard her coming and went to meet her. "Sybilla," he said. "I have only just returned. I was away on duty – or I would have come at once, as soon as I heard the tragic news. Permit me to tell you how deeply shocked . . ." His clear voice rang out like a bell.

"Thank you," she said. "Thank you."

"I saw your father before I came here," he said. "He told me. I met him on my way to my office, but as soon as I could manage to get away, I came. I wanted to tell you personally how deeply I regret the great loss you must be suffering."

He sat down on the chair opposite her. She looked at him. Once, when she had been a child, and they had happened to spend the season together in Venice, he had taught her to sail. A quick little boat . . . She had been frightfully proud and had boasted about it: that a real seaman was taking the trouble to show her how to handle a sail.

"You must be very lonely now," he said. "If I remember correctly, your mother and you were very close."

"Very," she said.

I must say something, anything, she thought. I must make conversation. He is such a busy man and he has taken time out to come and see me. . . . But her head was quite empty. She couldn't think of anything.

"I am working in a hospital," she said finally, "eight hours a day. And in the evening I am so tired, I can hardly feel or think anything, thank God."

She could hear a clock strike eleven. Time was slipping. How long would he stay?

"You mustn't cut yourself off from the world entirely," she heard him say. "You are young. Your mother wouldn't have wished . . ." Oh, certainly, certainly. . . .

"I don't think I could make myself care for people now," she answered. "I don't want to see anyone."

"I hope you don't refuse everyone," he went on. "Your mother's former friends will certainly want to be close to you now."

"They are very kind," said Sybilla. "But I'd rather my father or my uncle would see them. Besides," she added, with sudden bitterness, "there weren't so many. Mother had grown quite un popular."

"Yes," he said. "I know. War destroys even more unfortunately than one would think."

"That's why we sent out cards instead of publishing it in the paper."

"So you haven't seen anyone?"

She felt the penetrating gaze of his dark, blue eyes. She shook her head. "During the day I'm at the hospital." Her eyes were watching the time. Why didn't he go?

The part which was European in her, and ready to resign itself too easily to the sad things in life, began to give in to the fact that the man she had begun to love couldn't be saved, but, at the same time, the part which was American in her was still fighting and furiously refused to bow to the fact that she had been only a link in a series of disasters. The situation cried out to her personal individuality!

Come on! Pull yourself together! You're not licked yet! . . . He was saying something about being an old friend, and suddenly her heart began to beat and she could feel the palms of her hands grow clammy. After all, he was a man of importance. He might be able to help her. He might know somebody to whom she could appeal.

"Are you in very much of a hurry?" she asked.

so abruptly that he looked surprised. When he shook his head she went on quickly. "It's a great personal favor I would like to ask of you. I know I have no right to bother you with things like that, but if you could give me some minutes . . ."

"Go ahead," he said quietly.

"Maybe it is not even so personal," Sybilla went on. "It's a more general matter, concerning decency and law. You see, yesterday, a man was arrested. Oh, you must know about the bomb that was found at the Excelsior Hotel. Well, the police raided the quarters in which this man lived. When they tried to arrest him, he knocked them down and fled. But he was picked up yesterday afternoon and brought to the *questura*. It seems that the official there, a certain Signor Bartoldi, thinks that he is the culprit. . . ."

Was she telling the story right? How much could she tell? How much did she have to keep veiled from him?

"Yes?" he said. "Go on."

"I know the man is innocent."

She saw his eyebrows go up.

"You see," she said, "his father and my uncle were friends. His father died in the last war, in the battle on the Col di Lana. I know him. I know he couldn't have done it. I, and my uncle, Conte Rossi, would vouch for him. But Bartoldi . . . I went to see Bartoldi early this morning. He is ready to turn him over to the Germans for trial. . . ."

Now he interrupted her. "You want me to interfere, don't you? Well, Sybilla, I can hardly do that. The Navy and the police are very different departments. You will have to see someone else on his behalf, I am afraid."

"Yes. Maybe," she said. "But perhaps you can help me there. You see, I don't know anybody who could give orders to Bartoldi, but I thought you might know someone who could, somebody who has the power to interfere. . . . You see, the man I am speaking of shouldn't be tried at all, because he can't be held responsible for his actions. He has been confined in an asylum for nearly twenty-five years and has been just recently released—as a matter of fact, exactly seven days ago. But Bartoldi says that he has been released as cured, and that it is up to the Germans to decide if he is to be held responsible for his actions or not."

"What is your friend's name?" asked Claudio Torlani.

"Vittorio da Ponte."

"Vittorio da Ponte," he repeated.

"The Germans believe in eliminating everyone who can't be of use to them in one way or another," she murmured; "it's one of their principles. In a case like this his chances of being sent back to the asylum are very slim."

It was hard to phrase her fears so cautiously.

"Da Ponte," he said again. "Da Ponte from Verona. Francesco da Ponte. I knew him. We went to the Military Academy together, then I changed to the Navy. Francesco da Ponte . . . *Sì, sì.*"

She sat breathless, feeling her legs tremble under the thin material of her dress.

"I think you'd better go and see the Chief of Police," he said.

"I would have to ask you for an introduction."

He rose. "Yes," he said. "If I may use your telephone, I think I had better announce you personally."

Sybilla pointed to the small table at the other end of the hall where the telephone stood. She saw him walk over and pick up the receiver and she got up and followed him, quite unconscious of what she was doing, her heart still beating violently. She heard him say, "Admiral Torlani speaking," and then he must have changed his mind, for he went on to say, "*Bongiorno, amico.* . . . *Sì* . . . *Sì.* . . . Listen. I wonder if you could do me a personal favor. One of your men is holding a certain da Ponte. Yes. I know. I understand perfectly. It just happens that his father was a very dear friend of mine. Francesco da Ponte.

He fell in the last war. Yes. This man is his son. He went out of his mind as a result of head wounds he suffered, an eighteen-year-old boy, in 1918. He's been confined ever since. . . . Casa della Pace. . . . Correct. I just spoke to his doctor. He was released only seven days ago. The doctor is sure that his mind must have snapped again. Very understandable, I should say, coming straight back into another war. . . . *Sì*. . . . *Sicuro*. . . . I want you to send this man back to the asylum where he belongs."

He listened intently and his face grew harsh. When he spoke again, his voice sounded angry and surprised. "Am I to understand that the Italian police is afraid of not finding the real culprit? . . . I beg your pardon? . . . You aren't afraid of the Gestapo, are you? I think you're forgetting that they're our allies. . . . Well. If you can't protect an innocent crazy man from being shot, I'm sorry, but then I think the police department needs some men with more spirit. Badly! . . . *Sì* . . . I know. . . . I know. . . . No hard feelings, *caro amico*. . . . Your minister? All right. Would you be kind enough to call me back? Here is the number. . . . In twenty minutes? Yes. *Grazie mille*. I knew we would understand each other." And he hung up.

"I don't know how to thank you," said Sybilla.

He moved his hand through the air. "His father was my comrade . . . the duty of one soldier to the other. He's going to call back in twenty minutes. He feels that this is a too special case for him to bear all the responsibility alone. He is going to talk it over with his minister."

His face looked grave.

"Don't give up hope," he added.

He looked at his watch and then back at her. "I'm afraid I'll have to go," he said. "I can't wait for the call to come through. You take the message and in case things should be more difficult than we hope, call my office and let me know."

"Thank you again, so much, for bothering."

He bent to kiss her hand. "How much you look like your mother," he said. "Give my regards to your father and Count Rossi."

She didn't ring for Silvio. She saw him to the door herself and watched him get into the car which had been waiting for him. Then she went back into the hall and sat down on the big couch, leaning back into the corner, rolled up as if she needed all the warmth her body could give. She took her watch off her wrist and put it in front of her, on her lap. "He mustn't die," she told the time, "he mustn't die!"

Uncle Arturo came down the stairs, walked over to her and sat down. "I heard him phone," he said.

"I thought I'd better not come down, and waited till he'd gone. He is a nice man, isn't he? He was always known to be just and kind."

"Ten minutes more," said Sybilla.

They sat without speaking now, counting the minutes. . . . But I love him, thought Sybilla. I thought my heart was dead, but he has come and made me feel again. . . . She closed her eyes. For a moment it seemed as if he were really sitting next to her.

The telephone rang. She caught her breath. "You take it," she told her uncle.

But it was only a shop calling, that it couldn't reserve something or other unless somebody called for it immediately.

Ten more minutes passed.

"He should have called back by now," Sybilla whispered.

Suddenly she couldn't sit still any longer. She rose impatiently, went over to the desk and opened the box in which she kept her cigarets. It was empty. "Why don't they call back?" she said desperately.

"He might not have reached the minister at once," said Uncle Arturo. Again they waited.

"Do you think Bartoldi might have turned him over already?"

"I don't know, *carina*."

A church bell chimed. Twelve.

"I'm going to call Torlani's office," she said.

"Wait a little longer, just a few more minutes."

The minutes passed. The telephone didn't ring.

"But he should have called back by now!" she said. "Torlani gave him our number. And he sounded so hopeful."

Uncle Arturo said nothing. He knew what Sybilla was thinking — that Torlani didn't have sufficient influence.

He heard her take the receiver from the hook and then her voice, flat now with controlled emotion. "Admiral Torlani's office, please. . . . Thank you. He isn't in? . . . You don't know when to expect him back? . . . Thank you." Little sobs put into words.

He turned and saw her standing next to the table, the receiver she had forgotten to put back dangling from her hand.

It was about two o'clock in the afternoon, perhaps a little earlier, perhaps a little later — he couldn't tell — when Charles heard a key being turned in the lock. He didn't rise from the floor where he had lain ever since they had brought him into this lonely cell. . . . A priest, he thought. They would certainly send me a priest before they . . .

Two guards came in and looked at him curiously; then one of them said, "Get up."

Charles rose. . . . Breathe deeply, he thought. Keep on breathing deeply. . . . Who had said that? His teacher in Lawrenceville. "Whenever you feel you are going to lose your nerve, breathe deeply." He saw one of the guards flash something, then he felt the cool, strong iron of a handcuff on his wrist.

"Come on," said the guard.

As on the day before, he was marched through endless corridors and finally several flights downstairs; and then, to his great surprise, out onto the street. A prison car stood at the curb. The second guard left them and went to open the small door in the back of the car. Then he nodded.

Charles was pushed up the one small step and into the empty space of the prison car. The guard took the handcuffs off and pushed him farther back with a swift, rough movement, jumped back down on the street and slammed the door behind him, locked it. He heard them talk, the sound of their voices, but he couldn't understand what they were saying. Then, all of a sudden, the car started off and sped away. He was thrown against one of the iron layers of the wall and tumbled to the floor.

Inside the car it was darkest night. There was

no window through which he could see, through which light might fall. He felt along the walls for a bench. There was none. Then he sat down on his haunches, using the wall as a brace for his back.

Where are they taking me? he thought. He repeated it aloud. His mind was so empty it refused to work. Where are they taking me? he said. Where are they taking you, Vittorio da Ponte?

Charles Barrett answered him: *Well, old chap. I couldn't say. But maybe they think trials are a waste of time in this country. Anyhow, it would just have been a farce. Or do you think the Germans attach any importance to law as an institution?*

But they didn't give me back my belt, or my shoelaces, said Vittorio da Ponte.

He heard Charles Barrett laugh. *What difference can they make if you're going to die?*

He began to rub his head nervously. All the blood seemed to have left it.

Get a hold on yourself, he said. Come on, now. You're going to be shot and you know it. There may be something like a trial, a military trial. Some German officer will read the evidence, somebody else will read that you confessed to planting a bomb at the Excelsior Hotel, no matter whether you did or not. They may even add "while of unsound mind," to make it look nicer for the Italians and the Germans, and then the judge will decide that the best thing you can do is die, because you can't be of any use anyhow, neither to the Italians nor to the Germans. As a crazy man you just don't count. And they will march you up against a wall and want to tie your eyes and you will say, "Not necessary," of course, and maybe yell out "I am Charles J. Barrett," and the command will be given. . . . Well . . .

He let himself slip onto the floor and stretched out on the bare, dirty wood. Underneath him he could hear the wheels singing. Forty miles, he thought, or maybe we're going fifty . . .

Don't think of dying now, he gave himself orders. We all have to die sooner or later. It doesn't really matter, does it? It matters only for what we die. And you are dying as the most convenient scapegoat they could find. What a sucker! Instead of fleeing right away, instead of starting to escape the moment I reached Rome, I . . . well, never mind. I only wish that bomb had exploded. That would certainly make me feel better. What a dirty shame!

Don't think about that now. Think about America and what it stands for. The old pioneer spirit is coming back, it will carry us farther and farther, the old spirit which made us build the land and make it a land of liberty. It will last.

It will get stronger and stronger. And you have been a part of it and will remain a link in the chain, dead or alive.

He began to smile. Wyoming, he thought. I always wanted to spend a summer there, to see the Tetons, to see Yellowstone and Old Faithful. I promised to take Mom to Maine, to eat real clam chowder for once. Oh, to stand once again on the Triborough Bridge and look down at the river and the three boroughs, so different, and yet all a part of the dream we call New York! . . .

Sybilla, he thought. Coming home with Sybilla, sailing safely across the ocean, sailing up the Hudson by night . . . all the lights on . . . a magic mountain in the dark . . .

Where are they taking me? We must have been driving for nearly half an hour now? . . . Stop thinking about it. It doesn't matter, I'm telling you! All that matters is that you believe in liberty, that no man has the right to push the other one around. And it matters that there are millions of Charles Barretts who think the same, who still have ideals. . . . You are just one of these little men who are fighting for their ideals. And that's right. That's all right. That's quite all right with you, isn't it?

He began to hum to himself softly.

The car sped on and on. Then, all of a sudden,

it stopped. He heard the door to the driver's seat bang. . . . Voices again, muffled . . . and, after a little while, steps coming around the car to open the door for him.

"Get out," the guard called. "Come on."

Charles blinked into the light of the afternoon. How blue the sky was, how green the tall cypresses in front of him!

"Come on, Signor Vittorio," said Bruno's voice. "Here. Give me your hand. There we are. Now, follow me." He put his firm hand under Charles's arm. "It's all right," he told the guards. "Just deliver his papers and his belongings at the office. Come on, Signor Vittorio. I always did doubt that you'd be able to keep it up." And, chattering kindly, he led Charles up the staircase and into the back entrance of the Casa della Pace.

"The *dottore* should never have let you go," he went on, as they crossed the hall. "I told him I thought your relapse that day was more serious than he thought."

"And I thought I was going to die any moment now," said Charles.

Bruno smiled at him. "You mustn't think of things like that. You were always so easily depressed and afraid. Just keep calm. We won't let you die, Signor da Ponte."

He led him up the stairs. "The *dottore* wanted

to see you the moment you got in," he said. "We had a lot of trouble getting you back."

They stopped on the second floor before the door of Pederazzini's office. Bruno knocked softly. "Signor Vittorio, *Dottore*. He's back." And then, "I didn't know you were busy. Would you rather I took him to his room first?"

"It's all right," came Pederazzini's voice. "Bring Signor da Ponte in."

Opposite the doctor sat another man. "Da Ponte?" he said. "Did I hear right? I knew some da Pontes in Verona."

The doctor said, lowering his voice to a whisper, "This is the son." He rose and came towards Charles. "I am so sorry," he said gently. "You must have been through quite an ordeal. Well, maybe it is all my fault. I shouldn't have released you. But who ever could have thought this would happen?" He sighed deeply. "Are you feeling all right?"

"A little dizzy," said Charles. "Just a little dizzy."

Suddenly the man sitting near the writing desk spoke. "Is this the man you have been telling me about? The man you expected back?"

The doctor turned and nodded.

"Da Ponte, you said," the man went on. "Well, Francesco da Ponte was a great friend of mine. I wonder if you'd think it would be all right for me to talk to this young man?"

Pederazzini looked hesitatingly from one to the other. Then he nodded again. The telephone rang, and he took the call. "Do you mind if I leave you for a minute?" he said then. "There is a case in Ward Three that calls for my attention. You really don't mind? He is quite harmless."

"I don't mind at all," said the man.

He pointed to a chair and Charles sat down, moving it closer up to the desk. For the first time now he looked at the man, looked at the sun-tanned face, the dark blue eyes under the silver hair.

"I knew your father very well," the man said kindly. "I even knew you when you were a small boy." He smiled. "I don't think you remember me, do you? Well, I wouldn't have recognized you, either. But perhaps you can remember other names, names of friends of your family. Torlani. Do you remember Torlani?"

Charles shook his head. "No," he said. "I don't."

The man rose and walked up to the window, crossing his hands behind his back. He stood still for a while, then he turned. "But you should remember. Claudio Torlani. Well. Maybe you remember someone else. Giovanni Strada. Do you?"

"I'm afraid not," said Charles. Only now did he realize that he had escaped Bartoldi, the Germans, a farce trial and death, that he was safe, safe in the Casa della Pace, that he still had a chance. . . .

"But even if you don't remember him personally, you should remember his *name.* Giovanni Strada. Even then he was a very important man. He, and Giuseppe Martini. Surely these names must mean something to you. *Surely you would remember names of such importance.*"

Charles stared at the man. He caught his breath. And everything fell into its place.

This man wasn't trying to be kind. This man wasn't trying to help the doctor refresh the memory of a patient whose father he had known. This man was telling him something, something of the utmost importance. He was telling him the names! The names of those who looked upon the Americans as their natural allies. Those names would be worth more than one thousand planes or one hundred tanks. To know these names meant knowing the enemies of the Axis – the Italian Democrats – meant knowing that in certain sectors firing could cease so that his comrades could land without loss of time – without danger of life.

"Torlani. Claudio Torlani," Charles said. "Yes. Of course. You must excuse me. Sometimes my memory slips badly. That's why I'm here," he added, jumping easily and happily into the part of Vittorio da Ponte.

"I understand," said the man. "Your doctor told me. You certainly had a distressing experience."

"Claudio Torlani," said Charles. "Giovanni Strada. Giuseppe Martini." He reached over the desk for pencil and paper.

"Tino Pratti was a very good friend of theirs," the man went on, "and Giulio . . ." He spoke slowly and clearly and Charles wrote quietly.

"If I had only known that Francesco's son was confined here," the man said finally, "I would certainly have come to see him before this."

Charles understood. He had the complete list. He held it up to the light, reading it silently; his lips moved.

"One should always remember old friends," said the man. "A world without friends is not very enjoyable. You won't forget?" he asked, raising his voice. "You will remember, I hope. From now on, you will remember."

"I'll remember," said Charles.

He folded the small piece of paper which he had torn from the doctor's prescription block into an even smaller piece. The man came over to him, stood very close to him for a moment, looking at him. "You won't forget?" he said.

Charles shook his head.

The man reached out and took the small piece of paper away from under his fingers. "You see," he said kindly, "I am quite sure that very soon now you will be completely cured, and to prove how much I trust that your memory will get stronger and stronger and more concentrated . . ." He struck a match and held it to the paper.

"Don't worry," said Charles, and now he almost laughed. He felt like a man who has won a battle single-handed; he felt the deep, rare satisfaction of being useful; his mind, his heart, his body felt it. His life, his dreams, his ambitions, his suffering and his sacrifices and his hopes, were making sense.

He heard the doctor's steps echoing outside. "*Signore,*" he said. "Maybe you remember a friend of my mother's, the Contessa San Vigilio. I used to play with her little daughter when they came to Verona."

The man smiled. "I'm afraid I don't," he said. "The name, of course, means something to me. It is a very famous name."

"Would you give her my best regards?"

"I will," said the man.

The door opened. The doctor came in, followed by Bruno. "You'd better take the patient to his room now and see that he gets some rest. I'll see him later."

Charles rose. "Good-by, *Signore,*" he said.

The man held out his hands. "Good-by," he said. "I am indeed very happy to have met you." . . .

When Charles awoke from a deep sleep, his room was completely dark. He switched on the light, but there was no clock to tell him the time. He jumped from his bed and ran over to the door where he remembered the bell to be. He pressed it hard, and only a minute later, he could hear steps. Pederazzini entered.

"*Buona sera,*" he said. "Did you have a good sleep, Signor Vittorio?"

"Did you expect me not to, after the drug you put in the tea Bruno gave me?"

Pederazzini laughed. "I wanted you to get some sleep," he said. "Some good quiet sleep before . . ." He threw a bundle of clothes on Charles's bed. "Put them on," he said. "And when you are ready, take the elevator downstairs. I'll meet you in the hall."

He went out quickly, closing the door softly. Charles stared at the clothes. An Italian uniform, that of the Italian Air Force: bluish-gray and very similar to the British R.A.F. uniform; boots; a watch, a tag and a batch of military documents. When he was ready, he went on tiptoe to the elevator. Out of the dark hall came Pederazzini's voice. "Left. Follow me," and then, "To the right."

They crossed the big dining hall, went into a smaller room, through a pantry and into the kitchen; from there down into a cellar, and finally out of the building.

Outside stood one of the cars of the Casa della Pace. Pederazzini motioned to him to get in. As soon as he had closed the door after them, the car started and got away in the direction of the highway. For a while they drove silently, then the doctor said: "I had to be careful, even though I think all danger is past. You see, we don't have to worry about Vittorio da Ponte any more. You are just a soldier I'm giving a ride to. I'm sorry I can't bring you all the way. I'll drop you about a mile or two from the airport. You are going on a flight tonight. The pilot knows where to drop you. Report to Pilot Faustino, Hangar Eleven. A scouting plane."

Charles said nothing for a while. He was listening to the soft whizzing sound of the wheels. "Pietro," he said, then – "he never was crazy, was he?"

"That's beside the point," said Pederazzini, and coughed.

"I just wondered. He told me once that the sane people are sitting behind bars while the others run around and ruin the world."

"That's true in a sense, isn't it?"

"So your asylum is the headquarters of an underground movement."

"No," said Pederazzini. "There is hardly an organized underground movement here, although I must admit we live under very strange circumstances. The Germans try to govern us but they are not ruling us." He paused, then went on: "I would call it a conspiracy. Our history proves that we Italians have always been masters of that art, doesn't it?" He spoke in a bored, slow voice, as if he were discussing some medical problem with a colleague.

"I can't figure it out," said Charles. "God knows I have tried, but I don't understand."

"You are not supposed to."

"I was kidnapped, wasn't I? Straight from the receiving camp for prisoners of war."

"We couldn't think of anything better." Pederazzini sounded almost apologetic. "We went to a great deal of trouble. The doctor there is a colleague of mine. He got the post because he is a linguist. Well, for weeks he couldn't find the right man. He questioned every Britisher and American that was brought in. But the British – they never speak any language but their own; and the Americans had the most horrible accents!"

Charles began to laugh.

"What are you laughing at?" said Pederazzini seriously.

"I just wondered what made me keep up my Italian."

"Well, anyway, you were the right man for us."

He smiled. "Even though you didn't have red hair."

Again they drove in silence.

"Look," said Charles. "May I ask one more question? Why the hell did you try to confuse me so? Why all these fantastic complications? Why not, when you finally accepted me as the right man, why not tell me right away what you wanted me to do?"

He could see the doctor looking at him, shaking his head. "You wouldn't have believed us," he said. "If we had told you, you would have thought it was a trap for you or for the Countess. You Americans are not such credulous people. And you are not curious in the way we Europeans are. You are only interested in your own reactions, and you don't like to interfere with other people's lives. You had to be driven to do that. We were afraid that if we told you, you would just use the chance and the papers of da Ponte to make your escape, to go back to your company; and once you were out of the Casa della Pace, we had no means of retrieving you. . . . You see, we have to be very careful."

Charles didn't answer. The doctor was right. He certainly was a good psychologist. If he had been told, he wouldn't have gone after this mysterious affair but would have tried to escape.

"And then," the doctor went on, "we had meant to look you over. But when the Germans threatened to have the asylum evacuated and turn it into a hospital, we decided to send you away sooner than we had planned."

"And the Contessa?"

"We got the news of her death the evening after you left. You see, it wasn't published in the papers. They sent out cards. She died too quickly to give anyone a message. She was the go-between between Pietro and the man we didn't know. In case something should happen to her, this man would appoint someone to take her place and contact us."

"The man I met this afternoon in your office?"

The doctor nodded. "He didn't know until two days ago that we had found you and sent you to the Contessa. He had been called out of town on a special mission, and when he heard of her sudden death, he didn't dare contact us at once. We all had to wait and lie low for a while. As I said before, this is not an organized underground movement. This is a group of people who want Italy freed of German bondage, and want to end the war with the help of the Americans, their natural allies."

"Luisa San Vigilio was murdered?"

"We have reason to believe it."

"And why," asked Charles, "why couldn't you

send one of your own men to give this message to the Americans?"

"Not that we didn't trust them," said Pederazzini quickly, "not because we wouldn't have had a way to get someone out and over to your lines – but what use would that have been? The Americans would hardly have trusted him. The world knows 'Fifth columnists' too well and if they had they might have lost too much time investigating him. They may not even trust you; but they will give your story consideration, consideration serious enough to have their Intelligence service look into the matter and contact the persons in question. And you see," he concluded, "in the end it was all quite simple."

Simple, indeed! thought Charles, and he sighed. I will never understand Europeans, he thought, and the way they figure things out. I will never know what they call complicated or simple.

Again they drove in silence.

Seven days, thought Charles. . . . Seven days. And these hours may govern the fates of hundreds of thousands. . . .

"In a little while now," he heard Pederazzini say, "I will have to drop you."

Suddenly the general came into Charles's mind again. "Give my regards to Pietro," he said. "I'm sorry I won't see him again."

"Oh, but you will, one day," Pederazzini answered. "You certainly will. The day we will again fight at the side of our former Allies."

They had to stop for a shepherd leading his herd across the road. In the dark, the eyes of the animals were hundreds of green little lights in a black sea. . . . We are driving through the Campagna, he thought. Soon the marguerites will be in bloom. . . .

"Tell me," he said, "how did I get out? I had given myself up. I was resigned to being shot by a German firing squad."

"You very probably would have been," the doctor said placidly, "but the Contessina went to see Bartoldi. In vain. Then the man appointed to take the Contessa's place, who, by this time, knew that a certain Signor Vittorio da Ponte had been sent by us to contact Luisa San Vigilio, friend of that family, called on the little Contessina to pay his respects; and in her despair, she told him about Vittorio da Ponte. He happened to have some good connections and managed to pull a few strings – enough, anyway, to get you transferred to the Casa della Pace."

She helped me, she saved my life, thought Charles. She went to see Bartoldi . . . She . . .

"It's eleven-thirty now," the doctor said. "Your plane leaves at two o'clock."

That gives me time, thought Charles. . . .

"Don't try to get in touch with her," Pederazzini said. "Don't even try to phone. It would be too dangerous."

The car slowed down.

"Here we are," the doctor said. "It's about two miles in the direction of Rome. Turn right when it is time. You will have to pass a gate. Your tag and papers are in order. Better look at them in the meantime. Be careful, now. Very careful. You are just a soldier I gave a ride to, off for duty. Good-by and good luck."

He opened the door and let Charles out, and the car turned immediately and sped away, back in the direction from which it had come.

Charles stood and looked after it. Then he, too, turned and walked on quickly. After he had gone about a hundred yards, he could see the dim outline of a peasant house in a field, its low stone wall that surrounded part of the property. . . . I might just as well wait here, he thought.

He pulled himself up on the low wall, put roughly together with stones from the field's dried earth, here and there with a patch of cement, and watched the night spreading its dark wings across the country. Behind him everything was quiet except for the sound of water flowing into a wooden trough, the clatter of milk pails in a stable where the hooves of some animal moving in its sleep could be heard, and the cooing of pigeons dreaming on the roof of a barn. The thin light of a young moon lingered over the countryside, rising slowly, gaining more and more light.

Sybilla, he thought. Sybilla.

There was still time enough left before he had to walk the small distance to the airport. . . . He couldn't be very far from Rome. Through the night came the sound of a motor. A truck went by, its lights dimmed. There was no one to stop him from asking for a ride into the city . . . The next car that came along . . . I must see her again, he thought. I can't leave without holding her in my arms once more. We had so little, just the very beginning . . .

The cap he had put down beside him slipped to the ground and he bent and searched for it in the dark till he felt its soft cloth and hard brim. And at that moment, when he felt it between his fingers, he grew aware of the fact that he was in uniform – a soldier, again. He couldn't leave. He couldn't follow the desires of his heart, the strong urge of his body. He had to stay at his post. . . . And millions of other men all over the world are feeling the same way I do – wanting to hold what is dear to them to their hearts, once more: an old mother, a child, a woman – and not being able to do it. No matter for whom they are longing, they have to stay at their posts – and do their duty first.

If you were to go and she were caught, you wouldn't only endanger her, but everyone else, every one of those people who have thought and planned and sacrificed so many things to find somebody whom they could trust and send off with this message; not only these few people, but your own comrades who, by the very message you carry, may be saved a lot of fighting and dying. Charles Barrett, you can't possibly go!

The night grew darker and the stars brighter. His thoughts flew back to the day he had found himself in the asylum, ran through the seven days he had spent wondering and planning on enemy territory, went back to the hours in the lonely, damp cell. How strange fate could be! Here one group had taken all the trouble to build him up as Vittorio da Ponte, a crazy man, to help them serve their country, and another group had almost taken advantage of Pietro's ingenuous plan and used him, the very man they had laboriously created, for their own purpose – for the scapegoat they had to find to avoid trouble with the Germans. . . .

He smiled to himself. Maybe that was what life was, after all, the world in a nutshell: its two sides

— one where men built up, and the other where they tore down . . . And the only important thing was to know which was one side and which the other . . . and to be on the side which built up, no matter what nation or race. . . .

He glanced at the wrist watch which was part of his uniform. Under the metal screen he could see the lighted dial. Almost one-thirty. He slipped to the ground and started walking in the direction Dr. Pederazzini's hand had indicated. Through the dark around him he could hear steps echoing, to left and right, the small noise of bicycle wheels. . . . Other soldiers were headed for the airport.

After a while he heard the sound of voices and followed them. They were coming from the gate of the airfield. As he came closer he could see guards posted at the gate where the soldiers had to identify themselves, and a group of women standing there, saying good-by to their loved ones — mothers, sisters, sweethearts.

"Vittorio," said a voice.

He couldn't see her face, just feel her touching his arm. There were no words to express what he felt. He stood and could feel her fingers through the cloth of his uniform, touching him. "Billa," he said. "Billa." And he put his hand over hers.

All around them they could hear tender words,

the sigh which follows an embrace, the sweet noise of lips touching, here and there a crude joke and laughter, and the even steps of the military police patrolling the airport, inside and outside the fence.

"I am early," he said. "We still have some minutes. Let's walk away a little."

Under the next tree a boy and girl were standing.

There was a small ditch to the left of the highway and they sat down on the sparse grass, wet with dew, still green before the heat that would come and burn it.

"I didn't know what had happened to you," she said. "I . . . I . . . I didn't know one could feel that way. I didn't know I could. And then a message was left at the hospital, just saying that 'my soldier' would leave at this time from this airport, Gate Three . . ."

"Your soldier," he said, "is right."

He put his arms around her shoulders and felt them shaking. "I can't write you," he said, "I can't write you." His hands touched the stiff little cap on her head, the small collar around her neck, the brooch below her breast.

She didn't answer. He felt her lips brush across his face. "My love," he said.

She leaned her head against his shoulder. "I know," she said, "I know. Don't speak now."

They sat still, holding each other tight. Then he rose, "I must go."

They went back to the gate. From the sky came the drone of a huge plane. "Take care of yourself," she said, walking up with him to the line which had formed, "take care of yourself" — as every other woman was saying to the man in uniform standing next to her.

The ground lights from the port shimmered green and red through the night. "Come back soon. Come back safe and sound."

It was his turn now.

The guard reached for Charles's tag, examined it briefly, and flashed his light across his face. For a second he could see Sybilla's eyes and the tears which had gathered between her lashes.

"Come back soon," she said again.

"We will," he said as he passed through the gate.

THE END